Donal Holway

Susan Beth Pfeffer's many books for young readers include *Starring Peter and Leigh; A Matter of Principle; Courage, Dana;* and *About David,* which was an ALA Best Book for Young Adults. Both *What Do You Do When Your Mouth Won't Open?* and *Just Between Us* were named Junior Literary Guild Selections.

Susan Beth Pfeffer lives in Middletown, New York.

D1280197

Also by Susan Beth Pfeffer

FUTURE
FORWARD

Susan Beth Pfeffer

Illustrated by Andrew Glass

J
SF
Pfe

NORTH BAY
DISCARDED
PUBLIC LIBRARY

A 10-14

**Delacorte
Press**

q1

For Lew Grossberger

Published by
Delacorte Press
Bantam Doubleday Dell Publishing Group, Inc.
666 Fifth Avenue
New York, New York 10103

Text copyright © 1989 by Susan Beth Pfeffer
Illustrations copyright © 1989 by Andrew Glass

All rights reserved. No part of this book may be reproduced or
transmitted in any form or by any means, electronic or mechanical,
including photocopying, recording or by any information storage and
retrieval system, without the written permission of the Publisher, except
where permitted by law.

The trademark Delacorte Press ® is registered in the U.S. Patent and
Trademark Office.

Library of Congress Cataloging in Publication Data

Pfeffer, Susan Beth, 1948–
    Future forward / by Susan Beth Pfeffer ; illustrated by Andrew
Glass.
        p. cm.
    Summary: Having kept the secret that their family VCR can send
people back in time, eleven-year-old twins Scott and Kelly continue to
search for the best way to use that power and make an amazing new
discovery. Sequel to "Rewind to Yesterday."
    ISBN 0-385-29740-8
    [1. Video tape recorders and recording—Fiction. 2. Twins—
Fiction. 3. Science fiction.] I. Glass, Andrew, ill. II. Title.
PZ7.P44855Fu 1989   88-21829
[Fic]—dc19   CIP
                                                                  AC

Designed by Richard Oriolo

Manufactured in the United States of America

June 1989

10 9 8 7 6 5 4 3 2 1

BG

"It's great seeing you back at work, Pop," Kelly Forrest said to her best friend's grandfather as she examined the candies and gum in the display counter. "We missed having your store to hang out at."

"You shouldn't buy any of that junk," Pop replied. "It rots your teeth and doesn't do much for your brain either. Doesn't your mother have anything wholesome for you to eat at home, carrots maybe, or oatmeal cookies?"

"I eat carrots all the time," Kelly said. "I've practically turned orange from eating so many carrots. Besides, how are you going to make any money if you tell people not to buy your stuff?"

"Can she buy sugar-free gum, Pop?" Miri Weisberg asked. She was Pop's granddaughter and Kelly's neighbor and best friend.

"She'd do better to save her money and spend it on something important," Pop said. "A college education or the complete works of William Shakespeare. A quarter here, a dime there, it all adds up."

Kelly and Miri giggled. Pop sounded just like himself, and that was because of them. If they hadn't stepped in on that terrible day, Pop might not be alive.

"Am I late?" Scott Forrest asked, running into the store. "How're things going?"

"Late?" Pop asked. "Late for what?"

"For nothing," Scott said. "Just late in general. You know."

"I don't know, but I'm beginning to guess," Pop replied. "Is this some kind of conspiracy to make sure I'm all right? Are the three of you baby-sitters or bodyguards?"

"We just wanted to check up on you," Miri said. "You can't blame us for worrying."

"There was a robbery," Pop said. "It was almost a month ago, and the police caught the kid, thanks to you, Miri, and I'm fine. It's your mother who's the crazy one, making me go on a vacation, visit my sister Esther in Florida for so long. We drove each other crazy. Esther and I always did fight like cats and dogs, and the two of us stuck in that cardboard condominium of hers, well, frankly, I would have rather visited with my crook. He was probably a better conversationalist than Esther."

"Mom wanted you to get away, so you'd think about closing the shop," Miri said. "Retiring."

"To do what?" Pop asked. "Hang around watching

game shows? Thank you, I'd rather be a productive citizen."

"I don't know how productive you can be having nightmares all the time," Miri said.

"I told you there was no need to discuss those nightmares," Pop said. The kids could all see how angry he was. "I've had some bad dreams lately, that's all. The holdup was scary, I could have been shot, you could have been shot, naturally I have bad dreams."

"I'm sorry, Pop," Miri said. "I didn't mean to upset you."

"I know, sweetheart," Pop said. "These days I'm a little touchy. Here, why don't the three of you take your pick of this candy garbage on the house, and then get out of here and go home already. I managed fine all day while you were in school, and I'll close up early, I promise."

"You'll be home for supper?" Miri asked. "You know Mom worries when you're not."

"By supper, I promise," he said. "Now, choose your poison and get out of here. I have inventory to do. Who knows what the rats ate while I was making small talk with Esther."

So the kids each chose a candy bar, said good-bye to Pop, and left the shop.

"He has terrible nightmares," Miri said, in between nibbles of chocolate. "Mom's really worried about him."

"Does he dream he was shot?" Kelly asked.

Miri nodded. "Sometimes he wakes up screaming," she said.

"Well, he was shot," Kelly said, "—the first go-round, anyway—so I guess it's natural he'd dream it."

"I know," Miri said. "I just wish I could make the dreams stop."

"You single-handedly kept him from getting killed," Kelly said. "That's enough."

"It wasn't exactly single handed," Miri said. "If the two of you hadn't figured out the VCR . . ."

"Two of us?" Kelly said. "I figured it out. The two of you just followed my lead."

"Right, Kel," Scott said. Kelly could be a real pain sometimes. It was bad enough she was his twin sister; did she have to be two minutes older? And it was purely chance that she was the first to discover that the VCR their father had bought allowed you to travel through time as well as to record shows. If he'd had a little more time to play with it, he would have found it out for himself.

But no matter who made the discovery, it had worked out for the best. All three kids had used the VCR to travel back in time, but Miri was the one who used it for something important. And that was funny, since it was Miri who hated time travel and that strange whooshy feeling you got doing it, not to mention how weird it was when you saw your body dematerialize.

"I don't suppose the VCR could cure Pop's nightmares," Miri said.

"How could it?" Kelly asked. "Pop's dreaming about what happened the first time, when the burglar came in and shot him. I guess even though you changed things by going back in time, Pop still remembers how it was, even if it wasn't how it was, if you know what I mean."

"I know," Miri said, and then she giggled. "But I'd hate to have to explain it to anyone."

"What are his nightmares like?" Scott asked. "Has he ever told you?"

"He dreams the robber shoots him," Miri said. "Sometimes he dreams he's in the hospital dying."

"Well, that happened too," Kelly said. "Gee, I wish the VCR could fix things. Pop's too nice a guy to have nightmares all the time."

"Maybe it can fix things," Scott said.

"How?" Kelly asked. "You think Pop should go back in time whenever he has a nightmare and try falling asleep again? He'd have to come over to our house every night in his pajamas, and then he could go back to sleep and dream new nightmares instead."

Scott ignored his sister. He'd had eleven years of practice doing that. "Miri, do you think Pop understands about the VCR?" he asked. "About how you went back in time to the shop and kept the robber from shooting him?"

"I don't know," Miri said. "When it first happened, he acted like he did, but then Mom shipped him off to Florida, and we haven't really talked about it since then. Why? Do you think if Pop knew exactly what happened, he wouldn't dream about it anymore?"

"Maybe," Scott said, finishing off his candy bar and searching for a trash can to put the wrapper in.

"The fear of the unknown is a terrible thing," Kelly declared. "I heard that in a science-fiction movie once.

Everybody was worried about these giant tarantulas, only then, when they did show up, they *were* terrible. I think I'd rather be afraid of giant tarantulas than have one in my bedroom chewing on my leg."

"Kelly," Miri said with a shudder.

"How about if we let Pop travel through time?" Scott said.

Kelly and Miri stopped in their tracks. Scott grinned and walked over to a trash can. He deposited the wrapper and came back to the girls.

"You mean let him use the VCR?" Kelly asked.

"It's the only way I know to do it," Scott said. "Why not?"

"Why is the better question," Miri said. "Time travel is awful, Scott. It makes you sick to your stomach and it's scary, and what makes you think Pop would like it?"

"It's not a question of liking it," Scott said. "It's more like Kelly said, before she started talking about tarantulas. Pop's scared of the unknown. He knows he was shot, but he knows he wasn't shot, either, so he must think he's going nuts. And you can tell him the truth, that you traveled back to save him, but he's only going to think that's nuts too. Unless he does it himself, and then he can see just what happened."

"No, he can't," Kelly said. "He can't go back in time to the robbery. We can only travel back twenty-four hours, and the robbery was weeks ago."

"I know that," Scott said, although he had pictured Pop getting back to just the right time. "But even if he just goes back a few minutes, he'll understand better what happened, and then he won't suffer from fear of the unknown. Because he'll know."

"It sounds risky to me," Kelly said. "We're the only ones who've used the machine. What happens if something goes wrong and Pop gets lost in time? How could we explain that to Miri's mother?"

"He won't get lost," Scott said. "None of us ever has. We'll just set it for a few minutes, and then Pop'll be back where he belongs. And maybe he won't have nightmares anymore."

"Or maybe he'll have nightmares about dematerializing," Kelly said. "Pop's an old man. His molecules might not be up to it."

"Why don't we ask him, then?" Scott said. "Pop doesn't have to if he doesn't want to. But if he does it, it might stop his nightmares."

"He has been losing a lot of sleep," Miri said. "And I know he half believes in the machine."

"So let's give him a chance to completely believe," Scott said. "Come on, Miri. All we have to do is ask him."

"What do you think, Kelly?" Miri asked.

"I don't know," Kelly replied. "Time travel does make you feel strange, and Pop is pretty old. I don't know what it would do to him. But Pop does love doing new stuff. He goes on all the scary rides at the carnival, after all. Roller coasters even Dad won't get on, Pop's always first on line. So he might like it too."

"I guess we can ask him," Miri said. "If he doesn't want to, he'll say no. Pop's very good at that."

"Let's go back to the shop," Scott said. "And ask him

now, so we can do it before everyone gets home from work. Okay?"

"Okay," Miri said. "Come on, Kelly."

"Wait until I finish my candy bar," she said. "Maybe he'll give us extra ones if we come back empty handed."

"Kelly," Scott said, and gave his sister a push in the right direction. She pushed him back, and soon the three of them were running down the streets back to Pop's store.

A customer was leaving as they came in, and Pop looked up, surprised to see them. "You're back already?" he said. "You just left here."

"We came back for a reason," Miri said. "Scott'll explain it to you."

"Right," Scott said, and wished the reason were a little easier to explain. "We want you to come home with us," he said. "Right now, before our parents get home."

"I don't know," Pop said. "This is my first day back at the store. It might worry my customers if I close up that early."

"It'd just be for today," Miri said. "And your customers will understand. You shouldn't work too hard on your first day back."

"That's if you've had major surgery," Pop said. "Not if you've spent two boring weeks watching your sister Esther flirt with the mailman. What am I supposed to do at home, anyway, that your parents can't know about?"

Scott swallowed hard. "Travel through time," he said.

"Oh, sure," Pop said. "Time travel. Of course. Well, I'll just clear out the cash register right now so we can get going. Do I need a special time-travel outfit, or will what I have on do?"

"I thought you said he believed," Scott said to Miri.

"I thought he did," Miri said. "Remember, Pop, how right after the burglary, you said you believed in mutant machines, and that the VCR could let you travel through time?"

"Look, kids, if this is some kind of a game, then thanks but no thanks," Pop said. "I have a business to run here. Customers count on me. People buy papers here, and candy and gum, and lottery tickets. I can't just close up to go home and play make-believe with you."

"It isn't playing," Kelly said. "And it isn't make-believe. There were two robberies. In the first one you really were shot and you went to the hospital and they thought you might die. So Miri went back in time, so she could be here when the robber came, and she swatted him with her baseball bat, and you weren't shot, and you ended up going to your sister Esther's instead. Miri was very brave to do it, because she hates traveling in time, and even if she liked it, it still takes a lot of courage to go somewhere where you know there's going to be a robber with a gun. But she did it, and now she's worried about your nightmares, and I think you owe it to her to give the machine a try."

"Then it's true?" Pop asked. "I've had so many questions about that day, my memories were so vivid, but hard for me to accept."

Miri nodded. "I don't know how brave I was," she said. "It wasn't like I had any choice. I couldn't let you die. And now Scott thought that maybe if you saw that

the VCR really worked, you'd understand why you keep dreaming you've been shot. Because you were the first time, and that's what you've been dreaming about."

"The fear of the unknown is a terrible thing," Kelly said. "Only in this case, you have a fear of the known, sort of. I guess that's just as bad."

"I've never known you to lie to me, Miri," her grandfather said. "If you're lying now, it's the craziest thing I've ever heard of."

"I'm telling you the truth," she said. "You can go back in time through the machine. I did, and I saved your life doing it."

"All right, you've talked me into it," Pop said. "Let's give this VCR of yours a whirl."

CHAPTER 2

"The coast is clear, Pop," Kelly said. "My parents aren't due home for another hour. Come on in."

"They don't know about the VCR?" Pop asked, as he walked into the Forrest living room.

"Not that you can time-travel with it," Scott said. "You're the only grown-up we've told."

"I'm honored," Pop said. "It looks harmless enough."

"It is harmless," Scott said.

"It's better than harmless," Kelly declared. "Actually, it's the greatest invention in the history of the world. When people finally learn about it, I think I'll win the Nobel Peace Prize."

Scott sighed. The last thing he wanted was for Kelly to go into her Nobel Peace Prize routine.

Miri apparently wasn't in the mood for it either.

"Pop, time travel doesn't just make you feel sick to your stomach," she said. "It also makes you feel like you're flying."

"That sounds great," Pop said. "I've always wanted to fly."

"It isn't flying like that," Miri said. "It's more like you're stuck to the machine and your feet can't touch the floor."

"That's quite some machine you have there," Pop said. "It sends you through time and lets you defy the laws of gravity. I can't wait."

"I just think maybe you should watch one of us travel through time instead," Miri said.

"You mean I'd be able to see you back in time?" Pop asked.

"No, it doesn't work that way," Miri said. "But you could see us disappear."

"Thanks but no thanks," Pop declared. "I've been having enough nightmares without watching one of you disappear before my very eyes. Either I go myself, or else none of us goes."

"You'll love it," Kelly said. "Miri is the only one who doesn't. Scott loves time travel. Don't you?"

"Sure," Scott said, although he wasn't crazy about having his molecules flying around in dimensions nobody had gotten around to naming yet. "It's really easy, Pop. All you do is preprogram the VCR for a few minutes, and then you just hold on and go."

"Wait just one second," Pop said. "You know, when I was a kid, there wasn't even TV, let alone VCRs. What do I know from preprograming?"

"We'll do it for you," Kelly said. "All you'll have to do is hold on to the rewind button and fly."

"Sounds easy enough," Pop said.

"It is," Kelly said. "Pop, I hope you realize what an important person you are. You'll be only the fourth person ever to travel in time, and the first one to do it who isn't a kid. I bet you'll end up nearly as famous as me."

"I'm honored," Pop said. "All right. Let's get preprogramed."

"Let's do it for a half an hour ago," Kelly said. "When you were at your shop. That way you can see that you really do travel when you time-travel."

"I'll set it for five minutes," Scott said. "You need to be there just long enough to see you really did go, and then you'll come back here and have time to recover before my parents get home."

"Five minutes is really going to be enough?" Pop asked. "I wouldn't want to go back in time and not know it."

"You'll know it," Miri said with a shudder. "Pop, if you think it's going to bother you watching all your molecules disappear, then don't do it."

"Miri, you lack a sense of adventure," her grandfather declared. "If everybody was like you, Columbus would never have discovered America."

Miri looked mad, but then she walked over to her grandfather and gave him a kiss. "Have a nice time," she said. "Send me a postcard."

"You know you can bring stuff back from the past," Kelly said. "How about if you bring us back some candy bars from your store? That way you'll know you actually did travel through time. You'll have proof."

"And you'll have cavities," Pop said. "Okay. Three candy bars to go. No, four. I might as well eat one too. How often do I get to be the first person old enough to vote who gets to travel through time?"

"Just once," Miri said. "Are you ready, Pop?"

"As ready as I'll ever be," Pop said. "The machine is set, right? Now what do I do?"

"Make sure there's no tape in the machine," Kelly said.

"No tape," Scott said.

"Everything's preset?" Kelly asked.

"It's all preset," Scott said.

"Then all you have to do, Pop, is press the rewind button and hold on," Kelly said. "See you in five minutes."

"Five minutes," Pop said. He walked over to the VCR, paused in front of it for a moment, then reached down and pressed the rewind button.

Scott watched as Pop held the button and waited to see him disappear. Only, Pop kept standing there.

"This time travel isn't nearly as hard on the stomach as I expected," Pop said.

"That's because you're not traveling," Kelly said. "Scott, are you sure everything's okay?"

"It should be," Scott said.

"Let's do it again," Kelly said. "Pop, get away from the machine. Let us preset it again."

"Whatever you want," Pop said. "Miri, I don't know what you were making such a fuss about."

"Maybe the machine doesn't work anymore," Miri said.

"It still works," Kelly said. "I used it this morning. Scott, make sure there's no tape in the machine."

"There's no tape," Scott said angrily. "And I preset it right the first time."

"I never said you didn't," Kelly replied. "But this time let me do it."

"Be my guest," Scott said. He walked away from the machine and watched as Kelly pressed buttons.

"Okay, Pop, let's try it again," Kelly said. "Hold on to the rewind button and bring me back a chocolate bar. One with almonds, if you have any."

"Almonds it is," Pop said, and winked at Miri. He strolled back to the machine, saluted the kids, and pressed the rewind button. They all watched him do it. They continued to watch as he held on to the button and stood absolutely still.

"It isn't working," Scott said.

"We can see that," Kelly said.

"Maybe it isn't plugged in," Scott said.

"The clock is working," Miri pointed out.

"I'll check anyway," Scott said. He walked over to the outlet, and indeed, the machine was plugged in.

"How long am I supposed to stand like this?" Pop asked. "My fingers are cramping."

"You can stop," Miri said. "Either it happens fast or it doesn't happen at all."

"It's never not happened," Kelly said. "I don't see what could be going wrong."

"Well, something is, and I'm glad," Miri said. "I never liked the idea of Pop time-traveling."

"Pop, I really think you should watch one of us go," Kelly said. "To prove to you it works."

"No, thank you," Pop said. "If you kids want to claim this machine of yours works for you, fine. I'm not saying it doesn't. But I don't care to watch any of you vanish, and if I'm not going to get to fly, then I think I'll go home now and watch the news. See what's really going on."

"The machine does work," Kelly said. "Honest, Pop."

Pop nodded. "Fine," he said. "There are lots of things in the world people tell me work that I've never actually seen, starting with oxygen. I'll take it on faith. Now, if you'll all excuse me, I'm going home." He waved good-bye to the kids and walked out.

"I know it works," Kelly said. "It worked for me this morning. And now Pop'll never believe us."

"We should check the machine again," Scott said. "Just to make sure."

"I'll go back," Kelly said. "Just for a few minutes."

"I'm going home," Miri said.

"Miri, you've got to stay here," Kelly said.

"No, I don't," Miri said. "I hate watching you disappear. And I know the machine works. You don't have to prove it to me. Go, have a good time. I'm going to start supper."

"Call me later," Kelly said.

"Sure," Miri said, and left the house.

Scott watched Kelly preset the machine, press down on the rewind button, and disappear. He sighed at the injustice of life and went to the kitchen in search of something to eat. He settled for a banana and was just throwing away the peel when Kelly rematerialized in the living room.

"It's still working," Kelly said as she collapsed on to the easy chair.

"I saw," Scott said.

"This is terrible," Kelly said.

"Why?" Scott asked. "Just think how much worse it would've been if the machine had stopped working altogether. Can you imagine going to the repair shop and asking them to restore the time-travel function? I worry about that a lot."

"You worry about weird things," Kelly said, just as their mother walked in.

"You're early," Scott said with a start. A minute sooner and his mother would have been in for quite a shock.

"I left the office a few minutes early," his mother said. "And there was no traffic. What a pleasure. What are the two of you doing sitting in the living room like that? You look like the world's just caved in on you."

"It hasn't," Kelly said. "We were just talking."

"Talking's good," her mother said. "Homework is better. Have you started it yet?"

"Not yet," Scott admitted.

"Then why don't you?" his mother said. "The more you finish before dinner, the less you'll have afterward. And your dad said he was going to the video store after work to pick up a tape for us to watch tonight. So get started."

"Okay," Kelly said. She dragged herself and her books upstairs. Scott stood staring at the VCR, which he no longer understood. His mother was looking at him the same way he was looking at the VCR, and when Scott realized that, he blushed, grabbed his books, and ran upstairs.

Scott thought it was amazing how normal the evening was after their failure with Pop. The family had dinner together, talked about what had happened at school, at the office. Scott and his father cleared the table and washed the dinner dishes. Later, his homework finished, the VCR was set up with the movie his father had rented.

It was hard for Scott to keep his mind on the movie, and he could see Kelly was impatient too. His parents liked it, though, he noticed, and that was good, since otherwise they might wonder what was the matter with him and Kelly. Still, using the VCR made him nervous. It was like the machine was laughing at him. Halfway through the movie it was all Scott could do to keep from walking over to the VCR and kicking it.

Eventually the movie ended, and Scott and Kelly were told to go to bed. Scott, who usually was annoyed that bedtime was so much earlier than he wanted, was relieved. He went upstairs and changed into his pajamas. He wasn't surprised, though, when he heard Kelly knock on his door.

"Come in," he said, although she would have no matter what he said.

"Oh, Scott," Kelly said, and then, much to his surprise, she burst into tears.

Scott didn't know what to do. He'd hardly ever seen Kelly cry before. He supposed she did, but not in front of him. He knew he tried hard not to cry when she could see.

"It's okay," Scott said, although things didn't feel the least bit okay to him either.

"No, it isn't," Kelly said, sniffling loudly. Scott hoped his parents wouldn't hear and assume he'd done something to make Kelly cry.

"The machine works," Scott said. "That's the important thing."

"It doesn't work well enough," Kelly said. "Scott, what good is the machine if only we can use it?"

"It's still good," Scott said. "Miri saved Pop's life with it."

"But how many chances are we going to have like that?" Kelly asked. "I can't ask Mom to get mugged just so I can go back in time and save her."

"Are you jealous of Miri?" Scott asked. "Because she got to be the hero and not you?"

"Of course I am," Kelly said. "But that's not why I'm crying. Do you have a clean handkerchief?"

"I think so," Scott said, and after searching through his bureau drawers, found one. He handed it to Kelly, who blew her nose with noisy relish.

"Scott, you've got to know what trouble we're in," Kelly said.

"Trouble?" Scott said. "Pop isn't going to tell on us. And even if he does, what difference does it make?"

"Trouble isn't the right word, then," Kelly said.

"What I mean is I'm not going to win the Nobel Peace Prize anymore." And she began crying all over again.

Scott gritted his teeth. "Sure you will," he said. "Who else could they possibly give it to?"

"They'll think of someone," Kelly said. "Scott, if we're the only three people who can use the VCR, then how can it stop World War Three?"

"What?" Scott said.

"Suppose the President pushes the button," Kelly said, "and he starts World War Three, but then he changes his mind. We used to think he'd use the VCR to travel back and not press the button and then the world would be saved. But now he can't use the machine."

"So maybe he'll call you and ask you to do it for him," Scott said.

"Sure," Kelly said, blowing her nose again. "He'll call in his cabinet and say, 'There's nothing I can do, but I know this eleven-year-old girl who can prevent us all from dying,' and they'll all laugh in his face. You know grown-ups. They'd rather die than ask a kid to do something like save the world for them. We're goners, Scott."

"Maybe the machine will work for other people," Scott said.

"I've been thinking about it all evening," Kelly told him. "Here's how Pop is different from us. He's older and he's taller. So maybe the VCR only allows kids to travel through time, or maybe it only allows short people to travel, but either way the President isn't going to be able to unpress the button, unless we elect short presidents."

"There goes my sale to the Pentagon," Scott said.

"They're not going to want the VCR, either, if the only people who can use it are either short or kids. I don't think there are any short generals, and I know there aren't any kid ones."

"We have the greatest invention in the history of the world," Kelly said. "And it's absolutely useless."

"There go my millions," Scott said.

"There goes my Peace Prize," Kelly said.

"Maybe it's better this way?" Scott said.

Kelly laughed, and Scott joined her. Laughing felt better than crying, at least for the moment.

CHAPTER 3

"So how bad was Pop last night?" Scott asked Miri after school the next day. Kelly had soccer practice, and Scott could see her on the playing field, cheerfully whacking away at the ball with her foot.

"He didn't say a word," Miri said. "It drove me crazy."

"Well, that's better than if he told your mother," Scott pointed out. "At least this way she doesn't suspect anything."

"She knows something weird happened," Miri said. "She must. I spent most of last night looking at Pop, waiting for him to say something. All he did was look like he was about to laugh. Sometimes he just shook his head at me and acted like he was real disappointed."

"Do you think he was?" Scott asked.

"I don't know," Miri said. "I know I'm not. I never liked the idea of Pop traveling through time."

"Kelly cried," Scott said, seeing no point in mentioning he almost had too. "She figures she'll never win the Nobel Prize this way."

"She told me," Miri said. "I don't care. That VCR is dangerous. I know I used it when I had to, and it saved Pop's life, but one of these days we're going to do something wrong with it, and our molecules will never be the same."

"There's a lot of good we can still do with it," Scott said, wishing he could think of something.

"Just leave me out of it," Miri said. "I'm going to Pop's. Want to come with me?"

He didn't think he could deal with what Pop was likely to say to him. "I guess I'll just go straight home."

"See you later, then," Miri said, and she turned left, while Scott continued to walk straight ahead.

He kicked some stones and hardly bothered noticing how beautiful the trees looked with their leaves changing colors. It made him mad that the VCR seemed to offer so much and then didn't live up to its promises. Sure, it was fun traveling through time, but Kelly was right. You couldn't count on stopping crime every day of the week. And Scott had been counting on the tens of millions of dollars the Pentagon was going to give him for the machine. He'd liked the idea of being a multimillionaire before he started shaving.

"Woof."

Scott looked down and saw a big brown dog had joined him. It was definitely a mutt, part collie, he thought, with some shepherd mixed in. It looked a lot like Billy Greene's dog, and she was part collie and shepherd.

He checked to see if it was Billy's dog, but this one didn't have any collar on it, so he guessed it was a stray. Just the kind of dog Scott would like to have. Big and brown and friendly. His family had had a cocker spaniel for a few years, but it had died right around the time Scott's mother had begun working again, and she said it wasn't the right time to get a new one. The right time hadn't come since.

Scott wondered how his mother would feel if he brought this dog home. It was obviously a nice dog, and his whole family would like it once they got to know it. Of course, it would be Scott's dog most of all. Scott looked down at the dog and thought about its name. Somebody must have called it something. King maybe. Their last dog had been named Watergate, but his parents had named it. This dog, Scott would name.

"Want to come home with me?" Scott asked the dog.

"Woof," the dog replied. Scott wasn't sure how to interpret that, but the dog continued to walk alongside. Scott regarded that as a good sign.

He'd call it King, Scott decided, and King would sleep in his bedroom. He'd feed it and walk it, so his parents would never have to bother, and while Kelly could pet him sometimes, King would definitely be Scott's dog. He'd wait for Scott after school, and they'd roughhouse together. Maybe he'd teach King some tricks, playing dead and rolling over. Scott looked King over and decided he couldn't be too old. And he didn't see any fleas

on him. Fleas would be a definite problem in selling King to his parents.

Scott felt happier than he had all day. His own dog. His parents liked dogs, so they shouldn't be too hard to persuade. Kelly would be jealous, but maybe she could get a pet hamster or something. Besides, was it Scott's fault King had picked him? Some dogs just knew they belonged with certain people.

"Woof! Woof!"

Scott looked around and saw a car coming down the street. It was a pretty boring-looking car, and Scott couldn't see why King was making such a fuss over it.

"Woof!"

"Calm down, King," Scott said, but King ignored him and ran into the street, straight at the car.

Scott couldn't tell if the car knew King was coming at it, but even if its driver knew, there was no time to stop or swerve. King ran straight into the car, and his body was hurled into space. It landed a good ten feet away from where the car had hit it. The car kept going.

Scott ran over to King, and the other people on the sidewalk joined him. By the time he got to King, there were a couple of grown-ups already there.

"That car was speeding," a woman declared. "Today dogs, tomorrow kids. Reckless idiots."

"He's dead," another person said. "Never had a chance."

"Dead?" Scott said.

The man nodded. "Was he yours, boy?" he asked.

Scott shook his head. "We were just walking together," he said. "He didn't have a collar."

"I can see," the man said. "Just a stray. Well, maybe it's better this way. Winter is coming. That's hard on a stray."

"I thought maybe I'd take him home," Scott said, and swallowed hard. He didn't want to start crying on the sidewalk in front of strangers.

"I'll call the sanitation department from my house," the woman said. "They can take its body away."

"I was going to call him King," Scott said, not that anybody cared.

"Look, boy, the dog went fast," the man said. "There are worse ways to die. And he brought it on himself. He ran right into that car. So I wouldn't lose too much sleep over it."

Scott bit his lip. He hadn't known King long, but he knew him well enough to know the dog deserved better than a quick suicide. He deserved the same chance at happiness most dogs got. He deserved years of hanging out with Scott.

And he could have them, too, Scott realized. Saving a dog's life might not rate with saving Pop's, but it was a close second. All Scott would have to do was go back in time and hold King, make sure he didn't run into the street. And then King would be his forever. He'd invent some kind of story about how he'd saved King's life, and his parents would be bound to see that King belonged with him.

"I have to go home now," Scott said, not caring how he sounded. "See you."

"Take care, now," the man said, but Scott had already begun to run. He only lived a couple of blocks away, so it didn't take very long to get to his house. He fumbled with his keys for a while, and then he laughed at himself. He had almost twenty-four hours to save King's life. He could afford to take a couple of minutes to get a grip on his keys and use them.

He was glad there was nobody home, when he finally did get in. If Kelly were around, she might decide King was part hers as well. But once he told her the truth, she'd certainly see that King was his and his alone.

Scott tried to forget how King had looked flying through the air. It didn't matter anyway, because in a matter of moments Scott would prevent it from happening. And if King had the same kind of nightmares Pop suffered from, then Scott would just love him even more until he got over them.

Scott made sure there was no tape in the machine, and then he checked the time out carefully. It was seven minutes after three, according to the VCR clock. So King probably got hit right before three o'clock.

He paused for a moment, trying to work out the logistics. If King didn't get hit by the car, then they could both be home by now, but just barely. And it would definitely be best if King were in the house by the time Scott rematerialized. Scott didn't want to lose him again while his molecules were whooshing about. And while he knew you could bring stuff back from the past, none of them had tried bringing back anything that was alive, let alone alive and large.

So the best thing was to wait a few minutes, to give him enough time to get King into the house. Knowing that was the right approach drove Scott crazy, and he paced the house for five minutes, glancing at every clock he passed as he walked around and around. He knew King wasn't suffering, since he was currently dead, but it still felt awfully mean not to rescue him immediately.

Finally enough time had passed so Scott knew he had a cushion. He walked back to the VCR, checked his times out again, and set the machine for two fifty-five, with a return time of three-twelve. In those seventeen minutes Scott was going to save King's life and give him a brand-new home. King was definitely going to be grateful.

Scott triple-checked the times, took a deep breath, and pressed the rewind button.

No matter how often he traveled through time, Scott was always shaken by how it made him feel. First he felt as if he were flying. His fingers were attached to the VCR, but his legs were no longer touching ground. Then the entire world started spinning, which it probably was, he figured, and he was standing still. Or at least flying still. Then came the upset-stomach part that Miri disliked so much, and just when he thought he couldn't take any more of it, he was on the sidewalk, kicking stones and feeling mad at the VCR. Only, he wasn't going to feel mad anymore. Not after he saved King's life.

"Woof."

Scott looked down and saw the dog, his dog. "Hi, King," he said. "You're mine now. Did you know that?"

"Woof."

Scott bent over and scratched King's head. King looked up and woofed some more. Scott figured that meant King must like it. If King liked him already, he was going to end up loving Scott like no dog ever loved a kid before.

"You're a great dog, King," Scott declared. "And you're going to have the best home ever. What kind of dog food do you like, huh? Tell me what you like, and I'll see to it that's all I'll feed you."

"Woof."

"Okay, I'll feed you lots of other stuff too," Scott said, stroking King's ears. "I bet I can talk Mom into letting you have table scraps too. Of course, we don't eat much meat, but whenever we do, I'll see to it you get some. You'll like that, won't you, King?"

King paused for a moment and licked Scott's hand. Scott knelt by the dog's side and hugged him. King was the best dog ever, and Scott was the luckiest kid in the world to have the kind of VCR that could save a dog's life.

"Woof! Woof!"

Scott looked around, and sure enough, there was the car that had hit King last time. Scott stayed where he was and embraced King with all his strength.

"Woof!" King said, and tried to break away.

"No, King," Scott said, holding on to the dog as best he could.

But it was no use. King stopped woofing and started growling. Scott loosened his grip for just a moment, but it was long enough for King to break away and run into the street.

The car seemed to be going even faster this time than

it had before. And once again King ran straight into its path.

"No!" Scott screamed. "King, no!"

But neither King nor the driver of the car paid any attention to him. And once again the driver neither stopped nor swerved, and once again King hit the car straight on and was hurled into space one final time.

"No!" Scott screamed, and he ran to King. "No! No!"

The same two grown-ups beat him to the dog's body. "That car was speeding," the same woman declared. "Today dogs, tomorrow kids. Reckless idiots."

"He's dead," the man said. "Never had a chance."

He had a chance, Scott thought. *He did. I gave him that chance.* But all he could say was, "Dead?"

"Was he yours, boy?" the man asked Scott.

"We were just walking together," Scott said. "He didn't have a collar."

"I can see," the man replied. "Just a stray. Well, maybe it's better this way. Winter is coming. That's hard on a stray."

"I thought maybe I'd take him home," Scott said, but he could feel the tears coming hard, and there was no stopping them this time. He knew he couldn't bear to hear the man say all that stuff about how King had asked for it, so he began running, away from the sight of the dog he'd hardly known but had already come to love, the dog he'd promised life to, only to force it to die twice.

Scott ran to his house feeling as though his heart would break. He struggled with his keys to unlock the door, but eventually it opened, and he was able to weep in privacy. He broke down in the hallway, and kneeling on the floor, he sobbed at the memory of the dog and how it had looked at the moment of impact. Just a dead stray, he thought over and over. Just a dead stray. He was the only person in the world who cared enough about the dog to cry at its death. But the grief that Scott felt was as much as the world combined could have felt. And the tears he wept were tears enough for everyone.

And then he began feeling whooshy again. Scott realized with anger that he still had to return to real time. He'd gone back in time to save King's life, and King had died anyway. What good was the stupid machine anyway? It hadn't saved King's life. Pop was saved, but he had nightmares. Stupid, stupid machine.

And then Scott found himself standing in the living room, holding on to the VCR's rewind button. He broke away from it and collapsed onto the sofa. It was all he could do to keep from walking back to the VCR and throwing it across the room. He wanted nothing more than to see the machine fly in space and end up shattered, as shattered as King's mangled body had been both times.

CHAPTER 4

Scott had nightmares all night long, dreams in which he almost saved King's life over and over again, only to have the car hit the dog. Sometimes the car hit him as well. In one dream the car hit King, only it was the car that died, exploding in front of everyone's eyes, and they all blamed Scott, saying it was the fault of time travel and the VCR and he should be put in jail. Scott had never had a worse night in his life.

He hardly spoke at breakfast the next morning, but his parents didn't seem to notice, and if Kelly did, she didn't say anything. He hadn't told her about King. It still hurt too much. Scott wished he had some real symptoms, so he could skip school, but he knew he was perfectly healthy, or so his parents would say if he tried to claim otherwise.

Scott dawdled walking to school. Even though he made a point of not walking down the block where he'd met King the day before, he couldn't help picturing the dog and the accident over and over again. What he couldn't seem to forget was how King had growled at him, even though he was trying to save the dog's life. It was King's fault that he had died, but that didn't make Scott feel any better.

He made it to school just in time, and stood at attention listlessly as they all said the pledge to the flag. First period was English, one of Scott's favorite subjects, usually. But today he just couldn't get his mind to focus on anything except King.

His class was discussing a story they'd been assigned to read the day before. Scott thought he'd read it last night, but he could barely remember. He knew he'd done his homework yesterday, but none of it lingered in his memory.

"What do you think Eric meant when he said that, Scott?"

Scott turned away from the window when he heard his name called. "What?" he said.

"Welcome back to the classroom, Scott," Mr. Castillo, his English teacher, said, and the other kids snickered. "I asked you what you thought Eric meant when he said, 'Sometimes you run out of people to blame.'"

Scott tried to find the place in the story his teacher was talking about, but he wasn't even sure his textbook was open to the right story. He glanced at Betsy Isleman's textbook, to see what page he should be on, and found he was only one or two pages off. So he flipped the pages and then looked for Eric and his comment.

"Well, Scott," Mr. Castillo said, "we're all still waiting."

"I—I, well what I think Eric meant was . . . uh, what was your question again?" Scott asked.

All the kids laughed this time.

"Have you read the story at all?" his teacher asked.

Scott scratched his head and nodded.

"Then why don't you tell us what it's about?" his teacher said. "We're all eager to hear your version."

"Uh, Eric is this kid," Scott said, and tried frantically to read what was on the pages in front of him. He knew he'd read the story the night before. He could remember Eric's name. "And he, uh, he has kind of a problem."

"What kind of a problem?" Mr. Castillo asked.

Scott decided he no longer liked English class. "He hadn't done his homework," he said. "Same as me."

This time Scott's teacher laughed along with the rest of the class. "Not quite, but close enough," his teacher said. "Scott, I suggest you read the story a little more carefully next time. And try to pay attention in class. Teachers are a lot less likely to call on you if they don't see you staring out the window."

"Yes, sir," Scott said. More than anything he wanted to take his textbook and throw it through a window, but he knew he didn't dare. That was the absolute worst thing about school. Awful things happened there that made you mad and there was nothing you could do about it.

The rest of the day went just as badly. Scott kept

staring out windows and his teachers kept calling on him. Once, purely by luck, he managed to guess the right answer, but the rest of the time he came off sounding like an idiot. It was a good thing he usually did well in school, because otherwise he figured he'd get left back for the rest of his life based on that day's performance.

The final bell rang eventually, and no one got out of the school building faster than Scott. He waited around the school yard until Kelly and Miri came out, to see what their plans were.

"Hi, Scott," Miri said, when she and Kelly spotted him. "Rough day, huh?"

"Rough?" Kelly asked. "What do you mean, rough?"

"I goofed up a couple of times, that's all," Scott said. "My mind was on other things."

"Like what to do about the VCR," Kelly said. "I think about it all the time, but I can't come up with any answers."

"I don't think that was what was bothering Scott," Miri said. "Was it?"

Scott shrugged. "What are you guys doing?" he asked.

"I'm going to Miri's," Kelly replied.

"Can I come too?" Scott asked.

"Oh, Scott," Kelly said.

"What?" Scott said.

Kelly sighed. "It's just that Miri and I were planning on having some time alone," she said. "To talk about boys."

"Boys?" Scott said. "You mean like me?"

"No, not like you," Kelly said. "Real boys."

"I'm not a real boy?" Scott asked. At that point he wasn't so sure himself.

"Kelly means like Billy Wescott and Steve Delaney," Miri said. "Not real boys. Just other boys."

"Billy and Steve?" Scott said.

"See, now he'll just start teasing us," Kelly said. "Scott, Miri and I are practically teenagers. We like boys, and we want to talk about it privately. So, no, please don't come over. I don't go over with you every time you want to talk about stuff with Harvey Green, after all."

"What does Harvey Green have to do with anything?" Scott asked.

"Harvey Green has nothing to do with it," Miri said. "Scott, Kelly and I just want to have some time alone. Why don't you come over later. Say, around four-thirty. We can work on our math together then if you want."

"No, thanks," Scott said. "If the two of you don't want me hanging around just so you can talk dumb stupid girl talk, then you can forget about seeing me."

"Scott," Kelly said, but Scott had already broken away from them and begun walking toward the street. It wasn't like he even wanted to do anything with Kelly and Miri, he told himself angrily. They were welcome to Billy and Steve. They could talk any kind of dumb talk they wanted without him. He had plenty of other things he could do. He didn't need any dumb girls to keep him company.

Scott knew what he should do was go home and do two days' worth of homework, but that was the last thing he felt like doing. The problem was, he wasn't sure just what it was he wanted to do. So he kept walking around aimlessly, until he found himself a block away from Pop's store. Talking to Pop seemed as good an idea as any. At least he wouldn't want to giggle over Billy and Steve. So Scott walked the block and entered the shop.

"Thank you, Mrs. Clemens," Pop was saying to his customer. "And good luck."

"Thanks, Pop," Mrs. Clemens replied. "If I win, I'll be sure to give you a million or two."

Pop chuckled, and then, seeing Scott, waved hello to him. "Lottery fever," he said. "It always happens when the prize goes up."

"What is it this week?" Scott asked.

"Forty-two million," Pop said. "Forty-two million. That's a lot of candy bars."

"You mean if somebody buys the right ticket, they'll win all that money?" Scott asked.

"You buy two tickets for a dollar," Pop replied. "And you fill in six numbers from one to forty-eight on each ticket. So it's two chances for a dollar. Then if you pick the right six numbers, you win the forty-two million."

"Sounds pretty easy to me," Scott said.

"Sounds easy to everybody," Pop said. "Only, the odds are something like forty-two million to one against winning. Still, people like to gamble, and the state gets to use all the money for education. So I guess it's fairly harmless."

"Have you ever sold a winning ticket?" Scott asked.

"Oh, sure, lots of little ones," Pop said. "You pick four right numbers, you win a little bit of money. You pick five, you get maybe a thousand bucks. I've sold my share of four- and five-number winners. But never a six."

"Would you get anything if you sold a six?" Scott asked. "Like the couple of million Mrs. Clemens said?"

Pop shook his head. "All I'd get is the publicity," he said. "Of course, that pays off too. People figure this is a lucky shop, they come in to buy their tickets. I get a few cents for each ticket sold, and besides, once they're in here, they remember they wanted some magazines or a box of candy. I wouldn't end up forty-two million richer, but I guess I'd pick up a few extra bucks as a result."

"And people have been buying a lot of tickets today?" Scott asked.

"More than normal," Pop said. "But it'll get really hot tomorrow and Saturday. The drawing is Saturday night, and the closer it gets to drawing time, the more people decide to buy a few tickets. Well, I hope one of my regulars strikes it rich. Someone like Mrs. Clemens. The money wouldn't go to her head, and she'd be sure to help others out with it. No point just hogging all that money for yourself."

Scott nodded. "I'd give it away if I won it," he said. "At least some of it."

"You can't win it," Pop said. "You have to be eighteen to buy a lottery ticket. It's not legal to sell them to minors."

"Figures," Scott said. "Oh, well. I never wanted to be a millionaire anyway."

Pop grinned. "Have a chocolate bar, son," he said. "On the house. From the looks of you, you could use it."

"Thanks, Pop," Scott said, and selected a peanut-butter cup, which he devoured.

"Rough day?" Pop asked.

"The worst," Scott said, but before he had a chance to tell Pop why, another customer came in. Scott watched as the man bought his lottery tickets, selected his numbers, and gave Pop part of the card, while keeping the rest for himself. Scott couldn't help thinking that picking six right numbers just couldn't be that hard. You only had forty-eight to choose from, after all. It wasn't fair they didn't let kids do it. Of course, right then, not a whole lot seemed fair to Scott.

"I guess you're going to be busy all day," Scott said as the customer left.

"Busy enough," Pop said. "Why? What'd you want to talk to me about?"

"I don't know," Scott said. "About the VCR, I guess."

"Oh, the VCR," Pop said. "Have you figured out why it didn't work?"

Scott shook his head. "Kelly figures it's either because you're older than us or bigger. It still works for us."

"Pity," Pop said. "I would have liked going back in time. There's a lot I'd like to live over again."

"You couldn't do that anyway," Scott said. "You can only go back in time twenty-four hours."

Pop scratched his chin thoughtfully. "Twenty-four hours," he said. "Well, it's been quite a while since I've had a twenty-four hours I'd care to relive anyway."

"You can't relive the whole twenty-four hours," Scott said. "Just four."

"This VCR is a lot less fun than I thought," Pop said, but as another customer came in, he and Scott stopped their conversation.

This time the customer bought ten lottery tickets, and took his time filling out the twenty different games. Scott watched as the man pondered each of his choices before penciling in the numbers, and giving the stubs to Pop.

"He usually buys five dollars' worth," Pop told Scott as the customer left. "I guess he figures with the prize so big this week, he might as well double his investment."

"He seemed to know what he was doing," Scott said.

"It's just blind luck," Pop replied. "You either put down the right numbers or you don't. There's no system. Frankly, you'd do better to save all those dollars, put them in the bank, and use the money to pay for a decent education."

"But if you won the lottery, think of what a great education you could buy," Scott said.

"Education is what you put into it," Pop declared. "You can't just buy good grades. You have to work hard to earn them."

"Tell me about it," Scott muttered.

"What?" Pop said.

"Nothing," Scott replied. "Why wouldn't you watch one of us travel through time? Instead of just going home like that."

"I don't know," Pop said. "Maybe I didn't want to know for sure that that machine of yours really works."

"But Miri told you it did," Scott said. "And Miri doesn't lie."

"There's a big difference between hearing and seeing," Pop said. "Miri can tell me it works and she can even believe it, but that doesn't mean I have to."

"But why wouldn't you want to know the machine worked?" Scott persisted.

"Because even if it does, and Miri used it to save my life, the way she says, that doesn't mean time travel is something you kids should be messing with," Pop said. "There are certain things we aren't meant to have control over, and maybe it isn't right for anyone to have that sort of power. I don't know. All I know is I have these bad dreams, and I'm going to have to do something to stop them."

"Like what?" Scott asked.

"Your mother told me about this group for crime victims," Pop replied. "I called them up this morning. They do lots of different things, and one of their programs is group therapy for people who've been robbed or mugged. You just get together and talk about it, but I guess it makes you feel better if you see other people have been through the same kind of experiences. Anyway, there's a meeting tonight, and I'll be going. It seems worth a try. At least as much as traveling through time would be."

Scott nodded. "I hope it works," he said. "I had nightmares all last night too. They're no fun."

"Something happen to you?" Pop asked, but before Scott had a chance to answer, another customer came in. This one shielded her card from Scott, and filled her numbers out with fierce determination.

"I guess she figured you were going to copy her answers," Pop said with a chuckle when she left.

"You aren't going to tell anybody at the meeting about the VCR, are you?" Scott asked.

Pop shook his head. "It's your secret," he said. "It's not my place to tell people."

"Not to mention what they might think," Scott said.

"There is that," Pop said. "I'll just keep it to myself."

"I hope the meeting makes you feel better," Scott said. "Let me know if it works."

"I will," Pop said. "I figure I've spent enough time complaining, and not enough trying to make things better. Sometimes you just have to do for yourself."

"But what if you try something and it fails?" Scott asked.

"Then you just try again," Pop replied. "After all, if everybody succeeded when they tried, it'd mean we know the winning lottery numbers, and they'd have to stop the lottery. So it's good we fail at things."

Scott looked at Pop, but Pop just grinned. Scott grinned back. "I think I'll go home now," Scott said. "And try something easy for a change."

"Have fun," Pop said, and as Scott started to leave, two more customers came in to buy their tickets. Well, why shouldn't they try, Scott asked himself. Forty-two million was worth trying for any day of the week.

CHAPTER 5

Scott walked home from Pop's trying to decide what he should do with his life. What he knew he ought to do was his homework, but he wasn't ready. Pop had said a lot of things he wanted to think about, and homework wasn't the best thing to be doing when you wanted to think.

He also knew he could go over to Miri's. She and Kelly were probably finished giggling over boys, and would welcome his company. But he didn't want to talk with them either. He wanted to be alone.

Except that as soon as he walked into the empty house, he realized that, much as he might want to be alone, he didn't like the quiet. He needed noise. So he turned on the radio, but that wasn't it either.

Scott stared at the VCR and decided that he wanted

to watch a tape. So he went through his parents' tape library, only he'd pretty much seen everything they had, and the stuff he hadn't seen he didn't want to.

Scott plopped down on the sofa and kicked at a dust ball. It was so unfair. Here his family had a VCR, not a typical one at that, and there was nothing he cared to do with it. He certainly wasn't about to go back in time and relive that day's humiliations. And there weren't even any tapes he wanted to watch.

And then Scott remembered the hidden tape. His parents had been given an X-rated videotape by friends of theirs when they first bought the VCR. Scott's parents had immediately hidden the tape in their closet. Scott had discovered it within twenty-four hours. He had never had the chance to watch it all the way through, though, since he wasn't about to watch it with Kelly when their parents were out of the house, and he could hardly sneak into their closet late at night while they were sleeping. Besides, even if he did manage to get his hands on it while everybody was sleeping, there was always the chance Kelly would decide to get up for some time-traveling and catch him watching it. The Forrest family VCR got more use than most.

But he had almost an hour with nobody expected back in the house, and with that hour Scott could see the movie all the way through from where he'd had to leave off last time, and probably get to see the first few minutes all over again. Scott smiled to himself. He might not get much thinking done, but it was a lot more fun than homework.

He went to his parents' room and found the videotape

right where his mother had cleverly concealed it, in a box labeled PHOTOGRAPHS that also had two sex manuals in it. Scott had read those over and over for a long time, but he preferred the videotape. It had a lot more action to it. He took the tape, a movie called *Sinsational Lust*, went downstairs with it, grabbed some Fig Newtons out of the cookie jar, and fast-forwarded the tape to the approximate spot he'd left off last time.

Scott settled into the sofa, ate the cookies, and watched the bodies in action. A lot of what they were doing he had to puzzle over, and he decided his next chance, he should go back to the sex manuals and do some additional research. In a way it was just like homework, he told himself, taking a satisfied bite out of the last Fig Newton.

"SCOTT FORREST!"

Scott sat there paralyzed. In the eleven years he'd known his mother, he had never heard her quite that loud before, quite that shrill and scary.

"YOU TURN THAT THING OFF THIS MINUTE! DO YOU HEAR ME?"

Scott wasn't sure what to turn off, so he turned off the VCR, the TV, and the lamp on the coffee table.

"Now rewind that tape and give it to me and then you can explain what you were doing watching it!" his mother commanded. At least she wasn't quite as loud.

Scott did what she wanted. He turned the VCR on again, so he could rewind the tape, and then he gave it to her. She was standing in the doorway of the living room, and he could see the fury in her eyes. "I was curious about it," he said, as he gave her the tape. "I found it lying around and I didn't know what it was about, so I decided to watch it. I only just put it on. Honest, Mom."

"The only thing lying around here is you," his mother said. "You deliberately went snooping through my things."

"Well, if you didn't want me to look, you shouldn't have put it in a box called PHOTOGRAPHS," Scott said, starting to feel righteous. "How was I supposed to know I shouldn't look through a box called PHOTOGRAPHS?"

"Did it ever occur to you that a box I put on the topmost shelf of my closet, one even I have to use a stepladder to get to, was not meant for your prying little eyes?" his mother asked. "Foolish question. Of course it occurred to you. Otherwise you never would have bothered looking through that box in the first place."

"I'm sorry," Scott said. "I'll never watch that tape again. I promise."

"You'll never watch anything again, as far as I'm concerned," his mother replied. "Now go to your room and stay there until I lose my desire to strangle you."

"Sorry," Scott muttered again. He edged away from his mother and raced up the stairs. In spite of his mother he felt better about things than he had all day. He'd made it just about all the way through the tape this time, so if he never got to see it again, it was okay. Scott felt as if he'd finally accomplished something.

He knew he should do his homework while he was stuck in his bedroom, but it was hard to get his mind to concentrate on anything. So he just sat in his chair, looked out the window, and tried to worry. He knew he should, since when his mother was that mad, she usually took action, but somehow he didn't care. At least the VCR had proved it was good for something. It was an educational tool.

He could hear Kelly come in, and then his father, and he wasn't surprised, a few minutes later, to hear him knock on Scott's bedroom door.

"Come in," Scott said.

"I hear you bought yourself a mess of trouble," his father said, sitting on Scott's bed.

Scott nodded.

"You know what you did was wrong," his father said.

"Yes, Dad," Scott replied.

"Do you know why?" his father asked.

Scott thought about it. "I looked through your closet," he said. "Except I really didn't. It wasn't like I was snooping around looking for the tape. I knew where Mom hid it."

Scott's father tried not to smile. "At some point you must have snooped," he said. "I doubt that Mom told you her favorite hiding place."

"Kelly told me," Scott said. "She found it a couple of years ago."

"Great," his father said. "Do we have any secrets from you kids?"

"As many as we have from you," Scott said, thinking of the biggest secret he knew. If his parents had a secret that size, he'd be impressed.

"All right, what else did you do that was wrong?" his father asked.

"I watched the tape," Scott said. "But it was an educational experience."

NORTH BAY
DISCARDED
PUBLIC LIBRARY
PUBLIC LIBRARY

"*Sinsational Lust* is not an educational experience," his father said. "Scott, we keep certain things from you and Kelly because we don't think it's right or healthy for the two of you to see them. It's not arbitrary on our part. We don't want you to think what you saw on that tape is how married life really is."

"The characters in the tape weren't married," Scott pointed out.

"It isn't like dating either," his father said. "At least not the way it was when I dated." And in spite of himself he grinned.

Scott smiled back at his father. His father stopped grinning.

"There really isn't anything funny about this," his father declared. "You went through your mother's things deliberately to find a tape you knew we didn't want you to see. And then you lied to your mother about it. That's three things you did wrong, and frankly I don't see much remorse on your face."

"I'm sorry," Scott said. "I won't do it again."

"Forgive me if I'm less than convinced," his father said. "I know you just see it as a prank, but your mother and I both see it as something a lot worse than that."

"You're mad too?" Scott asked.

"If I had walked in on you, the way your mother did, I'd be just as mad as she was," Scott's father replied. "Is that clear?"

Scott nodded.

"Look, Scott, if your mother and I can't trust you to use the VCR in an appropriate manner, then we're going to have to get rid of it," Scott's father said.

"No, Dad!" Scott yelped. "You can't do that."

"We certainly don't want to," Scott's father said. "But your mother's had doubts about the VCR since we first bought it. She was afraid we'd end up spending all our time in front of the TV set, and she has a point. And now this. We're not going to make any hasty decisions, but we have to have your word that you'll only use the VCR in ways we'd approve of. And don't say you didn't know we'd disapprove of your watching that tape. You knew we would."

"I promise, Dad," Scott said. "Did you make Kelly give her word too?"

Scott's father nodded. "Now come on down for supper," he said. "And tell your mother you know what you did wrong. And then maybe things can get back to normal around here."

Scott followed his father downstairs and walked straight over to his mother. She was in the kitchen peeling carrots. "I'm sorry, Mom," he said. "I shouldn't look around in your closet and I shouldn't watch tapes you don't want me to watch, and then I shouldn't lie to you."

"Have a carrot," his mother said, and handed him one to munch. "Did your father tell you we're thinking about getting rid of the VCR?"

Scott nodded.

"It's a great toy," she said. "I love it just as much as the rest of you. But we can't let a toy control our lives. You do understand that."

"Yes, Mom," Scott said.

"All right," she said. "No TV for you tonight. I want

you to go back to your room after supper and do your homework, read a book instead."

"But it's Thursday," Scott said. "All the best shows are on on Thursday."

"That's why they call it punishment," his mother said. "Now go set the table and tell your sister supper's ready."

The Forrest family ate their dinner silently, and Scott was just as happy, when the meal finally ended, to go back to his room. He thought about turning on the radio, but he wasn't sure if that was allowed, so he just settled in, did his homework, and then read a book he'd taken out of the library a couple of days earlier. It was about a boy who traveled in a spaceship to the future, only he went about three hundred years ahead in time, and none of his time-travel problems were remotely like Scott's.

Everybody went to bed early, and when Scott was sure his parents were asleep, he slipped out of his room and into Kelly's. She was sitting on her bed, reading a book with a flashlight.

"I've been waiting for you," she whispered. "Come in. And talk quietly. I don't want to get into trouble just because you did something stupid."

"Sorry," Scott said, sitting down next to her. "Dad said they made you promise about the VCR too."

"I promised," Kelly said.

"Does that mean we can't time-travel anymore?" Scott asked. He realized with a start he wouldn't mind if it did. It would be nice to have an excuse not to ever again.

But Kelly shook her head. "I thought about it a lot," she said. "And I don't see how Mom and Dad could disapprove of it. Miri saved Pop's life time-traveling."

"Yeah, but that was Miri," Scott pointed out. "They never get mad at Miri like they do at us."

"But Miri never would have done it if I hadn't figured it out," Kelly declared. "I think it's okay for us to time-travel, just as long as we don't tell Mom and Dad about it. Let them calm down first, and then we can discuss it with them."

Scott nodded. "We shouldn't give them more than they can handle," he said. "It makes them nervous."

"An X-rated movie is enough for them right now," Kelly said. "Let's not push things. Especially since we don't know what to do with the VCR, anyway. Things were easier when we knew I'd win the Nobel Peace Prize with it."

"And I'd be able to sell it to the Pentagon for millions of dollars," Scott said. "Then Mom and Dad wouldn't have gotten mad when we told them."

"Story of my life," Kelly said. "Oh, well."

"Have you ever seen *Sinsational Lust*?" Scott asked.

"Sure," Kelly replied. "Not all of it, but parts. Miri and I watched it one afternoon, but we made sure to turn it off a half hour before anybody even thought about getting home. We thought it was pretty gross."

"I guess it was," Scott said. "But interesting."

"Very interesting," Kelly said. "Now get out of here, Scott, before Mom and Dad hear us and you end up in even more trouble."

So Scott left the room and made it back to his without

being seen. He got into bed, thought briefly of all he'd learned that day, and soon fell asleep, hoping he wouldn't be plagued by nightmares.

And he wasn't. Instead he had a dream that seemed to take hours to dream all the way through. It started with him on a spaceship, and it was going into the future.

"But I can't do that," Scott said to somebody else on the spaceship—Kelly, he thought, but maybe it was his mother. "We can only go back in time."

"How do you know?" his mother asked, and sure enough Scott could see they were going into the future. Only, then it wasn't his mother anymore. It was Pop. And Pop had King with him. King was barking and wanted to break free, and Pop was struggling to hold on to him.

So Scott got out of the spaceship. "He's dead," he said to Pop. "You might as well let him go."

"Dead's dead," Pop said. "I might have been dead, too, except for the VCR."

"Mom wants to get rid of the VCR," Scott told him. He looked around for his mother, but she was gone, and the spaceship with her. By now, they were in the living room, so there wasn't room for the spaceship there.

"Your mother is a very smart woman," Pop said. "Do you want a dog?"

Scott nodded. He looked around, and King was gone also.

"You'll need lots and lots of money to have a dog," Pop declared. "Money buys dogs. Money solves everything."

"No, it doesn't," Scott said.

"Money solves everything," Pop said again. "What if your parents get rid of the VCR?"

Scott started to cry.

"You won't need it if you have money," Pop said. "All you need in life to be happy is forty-two million dollars."

"But I don't have forty-two million dollars," Scott said.

"So get on the spaceship," Pop said. "And the money is yours." And then he disappeared.

"Pop!" Scott cried, and the sound of himself crying out woke him up. He stared at his clock for a moment, and saw it was almost two A.M. He sat up and tried to figure out what his dream was telling him, what it was he ought to do to get everything he wanted in life.

CHAPTER 6

Scott found he couldn't fall back asleep after his dream. He tossed and turned for what felt like hours, but was, he discovered when he looked at his clock, only twenty minutes. Twenty minutes in the middle of the night felt a lot longer than it did during recess.

He thought about reading some more in his book, but he was too restless to concentrate. So he got up, figuring a glass of milk might help him fall back asleep.

He tiptoed downstairs and was startled to see a light on in the living room. He thought it might be a burglar, but then he realized it was just Kelly.

"What're you doing up?" he asked her.

"Shush," she whispered. "Don't wake Mom and Dad."

"Kelly!" Scott said sharply, and Kelly immediately

raised her eyebrows and pointed upstairs. Scott made a face right back at her.

"I was going to use the VCR," Kelly said. "I was just about finished presetting it when you came in."

"Why?" Scott asked. He couldn't imagine why anyone would want to live through that day again.

"It's dumb," Kelly said, sitting down on the easy chair. "I forgot one of my textbooks at school, and I want to go back and pick it up."

"What do you need to do that for?" Scott asked. "You're not going to study any more tonight."

"I know," Kelly said. "It's just, what if Mom and Dad do get rid of the VCR? Then where are we?"

"What does that have to do with your textbook?" Scott asked.

"Nothing," Kelly admitted. "But I love traveling through time. If they do get rid of the VCR, then I'll never be able to again."

"Even if they do get rid of it, we might be able to convince them to sell it for a lot of money," Scott said.

"I still won't be able to use it," Kelly said. "You never thought about that, with all your big plans about selling it to the Pentagon. Why should the Pentagon let me travel through time? What can I do for them?"

"You could demonstrate it," Scott said. "Like selling Tupperware."

"Sure, Scott," Kelly said. "Anyway, one way or another, I might not have that many more chances to use the VCR. So I plan to use it every chance I can get."

"Even if it's just to pick up a textbook?" Scott asked.

"Even if it's just to pick a daisy," Kelly replied.

"You'll lose a lot of sleep," Scott said.

"So what do you suggest," she asked. "I do it when Mom and Dad are awake? You can't even count on Mom to stay at work anymore. She keeps showing up here early. She never would have found you today if she'd come home at her usual time."

"Are you going to be gone long?" Scott asked.

"Ten minutes maximum," Kelly said.

"I'll wait for you, then," Scott said. "I'll get a glass of milk while you're gone."

"Keep quiet," Kelly said. "See you in ten minutes." She walked over to the VCR, finished presetting it, and pressed the rewind button. Scott watched as she dematerialized, and then he went to the kitchen. A month ago if he'd seen his sister vanish like that, he would have screamed for the police, the FBI, and his parents. Now all he did was leave the room to get a glass of milk.

"What's going on?"

Scott whirled around and saw his mother standing in the kitchen doorway. "Hi, Mom," he said, and he nervously wiped away his milk mustache.

"What are you doing up?" she asked. "It's two in the morning."

"I had a bad dream," Scott said. "And then I couldn't fall back asleep, so I came down here for some milk. Did I wake you?"

"Something did," his mother replied. "I was sure I heard voices. Were you talking to Kelly?"

Scott tried to think what the best answer would be. He finally decided on the truth. "For a minute," he said. "She was awake when I came downstairs."

"Your father's the only one sleeping around here," Scott's mother declared. "Of course, he could sleep through an earthquake. Did Kelly go back up?"

Scott nodded and drank some more milk.

"I don't suppose you warmed that," his mother said. "Warm milk is supposed to help you sleep."

"I didn't know," Scott said. "It's just regular."

"I'm too lazy to warm it," his mother said. "Pass me the carton."

So Scott gave her the milk and watched as she poured herself a glass. He was glad he hadn't drunk right from the carton; his mother hated it when he did.

"What a day," she said. "What a week."

"Bad, huh?" Scott said.

"The worst," she said. "Job problems. Then there's your taste in video. And something else is going on around here. I don't know what, but I can sense something."

"With Dad?" Scott asked.

"With you and Kelly," his mother replied. "Care to tell me something?"

Scott shook his head. "Everything's fine with me."

"Sure," his mother said. "That's why you can't sleep at two in the morning."

"I told you I had a bad dream," he said.

"Any reason why you had it?" she asked. "Something the matter at school?"

"I didn't have a great day there either," he said. "I didn't flunk any tests or anything, but it was hard to keep my mind on my classes. I did my homework too. I just couldn't remember any of it."

"Maybe it's a full moon," Scott's mother said. "Oh. That reminds me."

"Of what?" Scott asked, starting to feel comfortable. It was good to know his mother was still speaking to him, and the milk was taking effect. Scott could feel his bed calling out to him.

"I wanted to tape something," his mother said. *"I Was a Teenage Werewolf."*

"You were a what?" Scott asked.

"It's a movie," his mother said. "And I've never seen it and I've always wanted to. Especially with you and Kelly approaching adolescence. And I forgot about it this evening before I went to bed. That's probably why I woke up just now. It starts at three."

"Three," Scott said.

"Three," his mother said. "So how about if I set the VCR and then we can both go to bed. And this weekend we can watch *I Was a Teenage Werewolf* together. It'll be educational."

"Okay," Scott said, and followed his mother into the living room. And the minute he did, he realized Kelly was somewhere in the past.

Scott had no idea what would happen if his mother reset the machine, because none of the kids cared to risk their molecules by experimenting. Two that morning didn't seem like the right time to find out either.

"Mom, why don't you go to bed, and I'll set the machine for you," he said, hoping his mother didn't hear the desperation in his voice.

"No, don't bother," his mother said. "You go on, and I'll be up in a minute."

"I don't feel well," Scott said. "My stomach." He groaned loudly.

"Your stomach hurts?" his mother asked. She looked skeptical, but at least she'd inched away from the VCR.

Scott nodded. Kelly was due back in about three more minutes, he figured. All he had to do was keep his mother away from the VCR for those three minutes, and then the rest was up to Kelly.

"You didn't mention it before," his mother said.

"It just started," Scott replied. "Maybe it was the milk."

"What was the matter with the milk?" his mother asked. "I had some and it tasted fine."

"I think it turned sour in my stomach," Scott said. "Maybe we should go in the kitchen and smell it."

"Are you running a fever?" his mother asked. She walked over to him and felt his forehead. "You feel normal to me," she declared.

"It was the milk," Scott insisted. "It had to be. All I had was the milk and some potato chips."

"Potato chips?" his mother said. "You got up at two in the morning and ate potato chips?"

"We were out of popcorn," Scott said.

"You're out of your mind," his mother said. "How many chips did you eat?"

"Just a few," Scott said. "So it was probably the milk. I really think we should smell it. It might be going bad."

"Fine," his mother said with a sigh. "You know, I wanted to have children. I thought they'd be cute when they were little, and entertaining when they were older, and a comfort to me in my old age. Nobody told me I'd be spending the best years of my life smelling milk."

"So don't smell the milk," Scott said, realizing that the milk-smelling ceremony would probably end exactly as Kelly was materializing in the living room. That wouldn't work at all. "Don't believe that I feel sick."

"Of course I believe it," his mother said. "If you say your stomach hurts, then it hurts."

Scott's stomach actually was starting to hurt. "Mom, tuck me in," he said. "I don't want to go to bed alone."

"Why don't you go upstairs now, and I'll be right up," his mother said. "I'll just set the VCR and turn the lights off."

"No!" Scott said. "Come up with me now."

"Scott," his mother said.

"I don't feel well," Scott said. "Mom, please."

"All right," his mother said. "But you'd better not be fooling."

"I'm not," Scott replied. "My stomach really hurts. Come on, Mom. Let's go up right now." He took her hand and started leading her away from the living room.

"Are you going to want me to sing lullabies?" his mother asked. "I really don't know that I have the energy for lullabies this time of night."

"Just tuck me in," Scott said, feeling like an idiot. He made sure his mother stuck to his side as they walked up to his bedroom.

"All right," his mother said as Scott climbed into bed. "Tell me about your stomach. Is it still hurting?"

"Just a little," Scott said.

"Well, we know it isn't your appendix," she said.

"That came out two years ago. I think it was probably the potato chips. Potato chips are bad enough at a reasonable hour. They weren't intended for two A.M. snacking."

"I won't do it again, I promise," Scott said.

"Good," his mother said. "Now let me go downstairs. By the time I get around to taping my movie, he'll be a senior-citizen werewolf."

"Can't you wait a minute?" Scott said. Kelly should just about be ready to return, he figured, and he doubted his mother was ready to see her only daughter rematerialize before her very eyes.

"Scott," his mother said. "What's going on?"

"Nothing," Scott said. "Honest."

"You only say honest when you're lying," his mother declared. "Did you know that?"

Scott shook his head.

"Mothers notice that sort of thing," his mother said. "You know, your stomach might stop hurting if you were willing to tell me the truth."

His mother was a lot more right than she ever dreamed of being, Scott thought. But even on the best of days it would be hard to explain about the VCR at two A.M. And this had hardly been the best of days for any of them.

"I think it was *Sinsational Lust*," he said. "You were right. I shouldn't have watched it."

"Oh, is that it," his mother said. "I knew watching that movie would be bound to disturb you."

"It made my stomach hurt," Scott said.

"Good," his mother said. "Maybe it'll teach you not to watch porn again."

"I promise I won't," Scott said. "Mom?"

"Yes, Scott."

"I saw a dog die yesterday," Scott said. "A car hit it, and it flew in the air."

"Is that what's upsetting you?" his mother asked. "How horrible."

"It was a nice dog too," Scott said. "Big and friendly."

"Accidents like that happen," his mother said. "But it's always upsetting to witness them. I'm sorry you had to."

"I love you, Mom," Scott said.

"Oh, Scott," his mother said, and bent down to kiss him. "I love you too. Good night, baby."

"Night, Mom," Scott said. He turned away from his mother and closed his eyes. He'd done his best for Kelly; the rest was up to her.

"Night, darling," his mother said, and she tiptoed out of the room. Scott was determined to fall asleep, but he could hear his mother walk down the hallway. "Kelly!" he heard his mother exclaim. "What're you doing up with your textbook?"

He couldn't make out Kelly's response, but he didn't care what story she came up with. He'd lost a lot of sleep and had to promise never to watch porn again, just to save her molecules. Which were only flying around time so she could pick up a textbook she couldn't possibly use until the next day anyway.

"That's it," he whispered at the wall. If they were only going to use the VCR for dumb little trips back to school, then there was no point keeping it, no matter what Kelly thought. The only one of them who'd ever used the VCR for good was Miri. He and Kelly had just squandered its powers.

"Let them give it away," he said out loud. Maybe the next people to own the machine would figure out how to use time travel for something really important.

CHAPTER 7

"Don't you ever do that to me again," Scott whispered to Kelly as they set the table for supper Friday night.

"Do what?" Kelly whispered back.

"Leave me there holding Mom off," Scott replied. "She was about to reset the VCR while you were picking up some stupid textbook you didn't need anyway."

"How was I supposed to know?" Kelly replied. "When a person gets up at two A.M. she expects to have a little privacy."

"Not in this house," Scott said. "Kelly, you can't just use the VCR for dumb trips all the time."

"I can do whatever I want with it," Kelly declared, her voice rising in anger. "I'm the one who discovered it!"

"Discovered what?" their father asked, bringing the salad in.

"Uh, discovered the mistake in the history book," Kelly said. "There was a mistake. It said the War of 1812 happened after the Revolution."

"It did," her father said. "That's no mistake."

"See, I told you so," Kelly said. "You can be so dumb sometimes, Scott."

"Dumb?" Scott cried. "You were the one who said it was a mistake."

"Please, no screaming matches before dinner," their father said. "It's been a long, hard week for all of us."

"I wasn't screaming," Kelly declared. "Scott, you put the knives on the table wrong."

"Fine," Scott said. "You don't like them, change them."

"I will," Kelly said. "Setting the table with you always takes twice as long. Daddy, why can't Scott set the table right?"

"Because his mind is on more important things," her father replied. "Right Scott?"

"Right," Scott said, and grinned at his father.

"Well so's mine, but I can at least set a table," Kelly grumbled. She moved all Scott's knives around. Scott couldn't see the improvement, but Kelly appeared satisfied.

Their father went back to the kitchen. "War of 1812," Scott said.

"It was the only war I could remember," Kelly replied. "I forgot its name was a date." She smiled at Scott.

"You could have ended up vaporized," Scott said. "Just so Mom could watch *I Was a Teenage Werewolf*."

"Tonight," their mother said, walking into the dining

room. "After supper. We'll watch it together and take notes. We've all been acting like werewolves around here lately."

"Not me," Scott's father said. "I've been acting like a vampire." He walked over to his wife and nibbled at her neck.

"I'd rather be a werewolf than a vampire," Kelly declared. "Being a vampire is so permanent. If you're a werewolf, you can still go to school and soccer practice."

"Watch out for games played during a full moon," her father said. "Not to mention finals."

"I'd like to be a ghost," Scott said.

"But ghosts are dead," Kelly pointed out. "What fun is there being dead?"

"You can haunt people," Scott said. "Follow them around and scare them all the time."

"You have anybody picked out?" his mother asked.

"I know I'm safe," Kelly said.

"How come?" Scott asked her.

"You don't even like hanging out with me when we're both alive," she replied. "You wouldn't want to be stuck with me when you're dead."

Everyone laughed. As Scott's mother made one final trip into the kitchen to bring out the chicken, the doorbell rang.

"I'll get it," Scott said. He cut through the living room and ran to the door. "Oh, hi, Pop," he said. "Come on in." He led Pop to the dining room.

"I didn't realize you'd started dinner," Pop said. "I didn't mean to bother you."

"We haven't started yet," Scott's mother said. "Would you like to join us? There's plenty of food."

"I already ate, thank you," Pop said. "I won't keep you. I just wanted to thank you for telling me about that crime-victims group."

"Oh, that's right," Scott's mother said. "The meeting was yesterday. How did it go?"

"It was great," Pop replied. "There were about eight of us, and we talked about what had happened, you know, the crime, and then how we felt about it. The people in that room had it a lot worse than me, most of them. And we all had bad dreams. Somehow, you know how it is, you think you're the only one with a problem. It's comforting to learn other people react the same way you do. And we talked about how scared we were, and how angry, and there was a social worker there who discussed what we could do to help us with those feelings."

"It sounds really helpful," Scott's father said. "Do you think you're going to go back?"

Pop nodded. "They suggest going for at least four sessions," he said. "It's really a great place. They're trying to expand it, set up a shelter for battered wives and abused kids, and they're also doing programs with the criminals in prisons so they can see what they do to their victims. Of course, they don't have nearly enough money, so I left a couple of dollars in their collection box. I guess if everybody they help out helps them, they might be able to struggle through."

"I'm glad you liked them," Scott's mother said. "I hope it helps with the nightmares."

"I slept last night like a baby," Pop replied. "Best night's sleep I've had in weeks."

"That's great," Scott's mother said. "Sure you don't want to join us for supper?"

"No, I'll get going now," Pop said. "I had a long, hard day myself. Everybody in the neighborhood was in to buy lottery tickets."

"Oh, that's right," Scott's mother said. "The big drawing is tomorrow."

"Tomorrow night," Pop replied. "I'm going to be doing business all day tomorrow, last-minute buyers. I even bought a ticket myself. Forty-two million never hurt."

"Forty-two million," Scott's mother said. "That could buy a few sweet dreams."

"Your supper's getting cold," Pop said. "See you tomorrow. And thanks again. I'll see myself out." And he left through the kitchen.

"Forty-two million," Scott's mother said. "I can't even imagine that kind of money."

"You could buy the world with it," Kelly said. "We'd be so rich."

"It isn't like that," her father declared. "They don't just hand you a check for forty-two million."

"They don't?" Kelly said. "Why not?"

"Because it doesn't work that way," her father replied. "They pay it to you over twenty years. And they take out plenty for taxes each time."

"It's still an awful lot of money," Scott's mother said. "It would pay for orthodonture and college educations and even a trip to Europe or two."

"If you won," Scott's father said. "The odds are several million to one against it."

"But somebody wins," Scott pointed out. "Somebody's going to win that forty-two million."

"Maybe not," his father said. "That's why the prize is so big, because nobody's won in a long time. They keep adding on the prize money until somebody finally gets it."

"I wish it was me," Kelly said. "I'd love being really rich. I'd buy us a castle."

"Do you know what it costs to heat castles?" her mother asked. "Buy us a yacht instead. We could cruise around the world, stop off occasionally at Tahiti or Buenos Aires. I'd wear nothing but bikinis."

"You haven't worn a bikini in years," Scott's father said.

"That's because I weigh too much," Scott's mother replied. "But if I had forty-two million dollars, I'd be thin. All rich people are thin. Besides, it's my yacht and it's my fantasy, and I can wear whatever I want on it."

"What would you do with forty-two million, Scott?" Kelly asked.

"I'd buy a ranch," he said. "With horses and dogs and a place for endangered species. I'd breed them, so there'd always be pandas and rhinos, and then I'd send them back to their countries and they'd never be endangered again."

"That's nice," his mother said. "Could I live on the ranch with you?"

Scott nodded. "We all would," he said. "We'd all help out with the pandas."

"What a great excuse to quit my job," his mother said. "I'd walk right in and say, 'Sorry, Mr. Heselberg, but I have to leave this job so I can feed some pandas.' Mr. Heselberg can feed the rhinos."

"What about you, Dad?" Kelly asked. "If you had forty-two million dollars, what would you do with it?"

"I don't want forty-two million," he said. "I don't believe in lotteries. They're a waste of money."

"We didn't say you had to buy the ticket," Scott's mother said. "Suppose you found it, the winning ticket, so you got the forty-two million without investing a penny. Then what would you do?"

"I'd buy some books," Scott's father said. "Hard-backs."

"That isn't enough," Scott's mother said. "Even if you bought a hundred, that's less than two thousand dollars. You still have forty-one million and change to go."

"I don't think anyone should be that rich," Scott's father said. "Money like that should be spread around."

"Great," Kelly said. "I'll take some."

"I'll come back for seconds," Scott said. "My pandas eat a lot."

"And I could use two dozen more bikinis," Scott's mother said. "It works out perfectly. You'll have your hundred books to read and I'll have a perfect tan."

"You're all crazy," Scott's father grumbled. "Pass the rice, and let's change the subject. How was school today, kids?"

After supper they watched *I Was a Teenage Werewolf,* which was pretty good, but not good enough to risk losing Kelly's molecules all over the universe. When the movie was over, they played Monopoly, until it was time for Scott and Kelly to go to bed.

"I hope we all sleep better tonight than we did yesterday," Scott's mother said. "Scott with his stomachache and me with my insomnia. Not to mention Kelly who felt she had to sleep with her textbook by her side."

"I was looking for mistakes," Kelly said.

"At two in the morning?" her mother asked.

Kelly shrugged. "I had a dream there were mistakes in it," she said. "So when I woke up it felt like I had to find them. The mistakes, I mean. In my dream, if you found enough mistakes, you won some money."

"This family's gone money crazy," her father declared.

"You're just saying that because you lost in Monopoly," Scott's mother said.

"I'm saying it because all this money talk makes me nervous," he replied. "It seems to me we're a happy family without millions of dollars. Why take chances?"

"I'd be willing to risk it," Scott's mother said.

"You've had a bad week, that's all," Scott's father declared. "Next week things'll be better. The week after that you'll wonder how you ever got along without working full time."

"I suppose," Scott's mother said. "I sure would like to jump ahead those two weeks, though. Come on, kids. The only thing I want you jumping into right now is bed."

"Can I read in bed?" Kelly asked.

"As long as you remember to turn the light off," her mother replied. "You, too, Scott."

"Great," Kelly said. "Good night, Mom. Night, Dad."

"Good night," they said back. Scott followed Kelly upstairs and used the bathroom once she was finished with it.

"Are you going to use the VCR tonight?" he asked her, when he knew they wouldn't be overheard.

Kelly shook her head. "You're right, I have been over-using it," she declared. "Besides, Mom didn't say anything about getting rid of it tonight. I think she figures it's okay if we all watch the junk she tapes."

"I won't use it either," Scott said. "What would you do with a castle?"

"Nothing," Kelly said. "I wanted to say I'd buy a spaceship, but then I figured Dad would say forty-two million wasn't enough money for a spaceship and besides, they don't make them real well anyway and was it worth risking my life just to travel around the universe when I could be using all that money instead to help the poor and the needy. You know Dad. It was easier just to say I wanted a castle."

Scott grinned. "I bet if Dad had forty-two million, he'd figure out lots of good ways of spending it," he said. "And not just on hardbacks."

"We all would," Kelly said. "Well, if you can figure out a way for us to win the lottery, I won't say no."

"Fair enough," Scott said. "Night, Kelly. Don't dream about any more mistakes in your textbooks."

"I'll try not to," she said.

Scott went into his bedroom and took out the book about the kid who traveled into the future. It would be fun having forty-two million dollars, he thought. Even if he shared it with his family and Miri's, there'd still be a lot left over. And Mom could quit her job, and Dad could read his books. They were a nice family. They'd only do nice things with the money.

He propped up his pillow and tried reading the book, but the thought of all that money just waiting for some-one to claim it kept him from reading. There had to be a way for him to win the lottery. Some system. Some trick.

And then Scott put his book down with a thud. He knew the trick, the system. It might not work, and the risk was great. But if it did, his family would be forty-two million dollars richer by Sunday.

CHAPTER 8

It was one thing to know what to do. It was quite another to know how to do it.

Timing was crucial, Scott knew. There were two different possibilities, but the problem was, they both had real risks and drawbacks.

He wished he could wake Kelly up and discuss it with her, but he was afraid she might talk him out of it. Besides, the fewer people who knew the better. It was crucial his parents never find out. And Kelly was perfectly capable of telling them just to score points. Even with forty-two million dollars at stake, Kelly could be petty.

Scott sat up in bed, trying to work things out in the middle of the night, in a completely dark room, with his body crying out for some sleep. To win the lottery he had to know the winning numbers. And they shouldn't be that hard to find out. The papers always listed the winning numbers the morning after the drawing. The drawing was Saturday night, so the Sunday-morning papers would have the winning numbers.

The question was, should Scott wait until Sunday morning, find out the winning numbers, and then go back in time to Saturday to buy the ticket?

Or should he risk everything and see if the VCR could send him into the future, so he could find out the numbers before they were actually drawn?

Ordinarily, Scott would wait until Sunday and do it in reverse, the way he was used to. Going back had worked for Miri, after all. She'd traveled back in time and changed things for the better.

But this was the lottery. Millions bought tickets, thousands of shop owners sold them, and hundreds of state employees worked on it as well. Scott couldn't be sure what would happen if he changed the past on so many people. Probably nothing, but it didn't feel right to him.

Besides, if he went to the future and it didn't work out, he'd still have the past to change things. If he waited until Sunday and his plan fell through, his family was doomed to a lifetime of poverty.

And finally, Scott wanted to do something as brave and daring with the VCR as Kelly and Miri. Sure, when Kelly first went back in time, it was an accident, but once she'd realized what she'd done, she'd proved her courage by doing it again intentionally. And Miri had risked her life going back and stopping the robbery. And what had Scott done? He'd just traveled back in time to relive his mistakes. He couldn't even hold on to a dog long enough to keep it from getting hit by a car. For him the VCR had been a total waste.

But traveling to the future would really be something. And even if the lottery plan failed, he could still sell the VCR to the Pentagon. They'd be thrilled to have a machine that would tell them the future, even if they did have to employ a short person to do the actual traveling. His fortune would be made.

It was nerve wracking to wait for the right time to try the VCR. Scott had twenty-four hours to play with, but there was no point going ahead in time before the papers were out. And that meant there was no point using the VCR much before six A.M., which was four hours away.

But he was scared he would oversleep. Scott couldn't use the VCR if anyone else was awake. He needed to have enough time, too, to find out the winning numbers, and then persuade someone, his mother probably, to buy the ticket for him. His father would probably be impossible to budge, but his mother might invest a dollar on the off chance her dreams of Tahiti and bikinis might come true.

Scott decided not to set his alarm, since it might wake someone up when it went off. Kelly, probably, and she'd know something was going on and insist on being involved. And that was exactly what Scott wanted to avoid.

Why were things so complicated for him? It seemed so easy for the rest of the world. When it wanted to try something risky and daring, it just did it. But for Scott there were endless details to deal with. It just wasn't fair.

Then Scott remembered his father's internal alarm

clock system. When he had to get up in the morning, he'd just say the time he wanted to wake up over and over again, and then, he claimed, his internal alarm clock was set, and he'd wake up naturally at the right hour. It didn't sound foolproof to Scott, but his choices were limited. So he whispered six A.M. to himself over and over again, before falling asleep. And it worked. Granted, he woke up at three A.M., four A.M., five A.M., and five-thirty A.M. as well, but at least he woke up at six. And when he did wake up, he was wide awake. He was a man with a destination, and the time had come to see if he could reach it.

Scott climbed out of bed and got dressed as quietly as he could. He didn't want to face the future in his pajamas. Then he tiptoed out of his room and went downstairs. He died each time a stair squeaked, but no one else seemed to hear. By the time he made it to the living room he was shaking. He was also famished, but there was no time to eat. Besides, if traveling into the future was even slightly worse than traveling into the past, it was best done on an empty stomach.

It was six-ten on the digital clock. Scott had an hour to play with, but Kelly sometimes woke up early, even on Saturday mornings. So it was now or never, and he could only hope he'd find a paper that early in the morning.

Scott preset the VCR to five forty-five A.M. He wished he had more than twenty-five minutes, but he didn't, so he set the machine for those twenty-five minutes. Then he made sure there was no tape in the machine. When he saw there wasn't, he clenched his fists, closed his eyes, and prayed that his molecules wouldn't end up destroyed all over the universe. Then, with more courage than he'd ever known he had, he put his fingers on the fast-forward button and pressed as hard as he could.

WHOOSH!

Scott was used to time-travel sensations, the feeling of floating, of looking down and watching your body become transparent, but this was something else. When you went back in time, everything seemed to take forever. This time he felt speed and compression, like a spring being wound tight. Then he felt like boiling water, not the heat so much as the sensation of bubbling. His molecules seemed to be bouncing against each other, and everything was moving too fast for him to look down and watch himself disappear. Whatever was going on, it was different and scary and exciting.

At last Scott found himself standing in the living room just as if nothing had happened. He blinked and looked around, trying to figure things out. Maybe nothing had happened.

But he'd come up with a system to prove to himself that he had indeed traveled to Sunday. Scott forced himself to walk to the kitchen, and found Saturday's paper on the kitchen counter, where his mother inevitably left it. Scott picked it up and with trembling hands, opened it to the crossword puzzle. Sure enough, his mother had filled it out. That could only mean it was Sunday, and Scott was twenty-four hours ahead of the world.

He felt like jumping up and down, only there was no time for celebrating. So instead he went to the front door, to see if by some miracle the paper had already arrived.

Only, of course it hadn't; it was too early. It was one thing to travel ahead in time, Scott found, and quite another to get the information he needed.

So Scott put on his jacket and left the house. Somewhere there was a Sunday paper for him to look at. Then he'd memorize the numbers. Scott didn't want to risk carrying them back with him. The less evidence of what he was doing, the better. If he ever wanted to prove that the VCR did let you travel to the future, there would be safer ways of demonstrating it.

His first thought was to go to Pop's store. Pop opened at six, but he would be there already, assembling the papers for his first customers. But Scott didn't want Pop to see him up so early in the morning. Pop was the only grown-up who might figure things out, and the less he knew the better.

The diner! There was an all-night diner five blocks away from the Forrest house, and it sold papers. Scott began running toward the diner.

He found he liked being out that early. The world felt different. It was still dark, but there was the promise of dawn in the sky. There was no traffic, and only the very rare light shining in someone's house, and the sound of a dog, disturbed by Scott's activity, barking nearby, let Scott know the world was shared by other people. Scott loved the feeling of having a head start on the universe. Not just an hour's head start either. Scott was almost twenty-four hours ahead of all those sleeping people, twenty-four hours that he'd live again, knowing what was going to be. Scott was so overwhelmed with his feelings of power that for a moment he felt he could fly. But when he tried it, running so fast that he was sure he would take off and skim across the streets, he tripped on takeoff and fell flat on the pavement.

Scott couldn't believe how stupid he was being, risking forty-two million dollars on the fantasy of being a bird. He checked himself out and found nothing broken, except a few of his dumber dreams. The VCR was amazing enough even without flying. Besides, the Pentagon could always borrow a plane from the Air Force if it really wanted to fly. Scott wasn't positive how it worked, but he thought the Pentagon owned the Air Force and could use its planes anytime it wanted.

He slowed down at the diner, so he'd seem less conspicuous. Scott straightened himself out and walked into the diner. He was surprised to see it was already full of people eating an early breakfast.

"How many?" the cashier asked him.

"How many what?" Scott replied.

"How many for breakfast?" the cashier said. "Are you here alone or are your parents with you?"

"I just want to look at the paper," Scott told her. "That's tomorrow's, I mean today's, paper, right?"

"You want to buy it, it's one dollar," the cashier told him.

Scott checked his jacket pocket and found a quarter and a dime. Sunday was allowance day, so it was no surprise to find he was close to bankrupt. "I don't have a dollar," he said.

"There's a two-dollar minimum," the cashier declared. "Why don't you go someplace else to hang out?"

"Okay," Scott said, taking a longing look at the papers

on the counter. "Can't I take one quick look? Then I promise I'll go."

"Get out of here before I call the manager and he throws you out," the cashier said.

"I'm going," Scott muttered, and left the diner. When he was worth forty-two million, he vowed, he'd buy the diner and fire the cashier. How would it have hurt to let him look at the papers?

Righteous indignation was fine, but it wasn't telling him what he needed to know, and Scott didn't have time to waste. He remembered the little grocery store a block away from the diner. It was probably open, and the people there were nicer than the ones at the diner.

Scott ran the block to the grocery and got there as it was opening. Scott waved hello to the store's owner.

"You're up early," the grocer said to him.

"I need to look at the paper," Scott replied. "If I give you a quarter, would you let me take a look?"

The grocer chuckled. "Want to pay a rental fee, huh?" he said. "Sure, why not. You promise you won't rip it up or anything?"

"I promise," Scott said, handing over the quarter. "I just need to check something out." He lifted the paper from the top of the pile and tried to find the winning lottery ticket number.

"What're you looking for?" the grocer asked him. "The baseball scores are on the back page."

"No, I want the lottery ticket numbers," Scott replied. "I, I mean my mother, bought a ticket yesterday, and I think she picked the right numbers. I want to see for sure."

"I don't blame you," the grocer said. "That'd be on page three. There was a big story about it. So many people bought tickets, the prize went up to forty-five million."

"Forty-five million!" Scott yelped. At that very moment he was two steps away from being a forty-five millionaire. He was so excited, it was hard to find page three.

But there it was, and in a nice, easy-to-find box, were the winning numbers. Two, eight, nine, seventeen, forty-four, and forty-eight. Six numbers that meant forty-five million dollars.

"Well, boy?" the grocer asked. "Are those your mother's numbers?"

"I don't know," Scott said. "I didn't write Mom's down. These look right, though."

"Even if she just got four right, she'll get a prize," the grocer said. "Here, let me get you a piece of paper, and you can write the winning numbers down."

"No, that's okay, I'll just memorize them," Scott said. "Two, eight, nine, seventeen, forty-four, and forty-eight." He repeated them five times, to make sure he had them straight.

"Whatever you want," the grocer said. "Good luck. I've always wanted to meet a winner."

"I may not be one," Scott said. "Thanks again."

"No problem," the grocer said. "Here, take your quarter back. Remember me if you strike it rich."

"Great," Scott said. He checked the numbers out one more time and then began the run back to his house. He made it back with only a couple of minutes to spare.

"Two, eight, nine, seventeen, forty-four, forty-eight," he said over and over again, until the whooshy sensation returned with a vengeance. Scott longed for something to hold on to, but he didn't have the strength to grab for a chair. Instead his body began boiling again, his molecules jumping all over the place, and he found he was being propelled out of where he was into a void, a dark terrifying void, and then almost before he had a chance to blink his eyes, count his arms and legs, and grab his flying molecules, Scott found himself standing in front of the VCR, his body shaking and his fingers pressed firmly against the fast-forward button.

For a minute Scott stood absolutely still, not daring to move away from the button. It took him a minute to regain all his body sensations anyway. Wherever his molecules had been, they were in no hurry to get back to their normal places. Scott knew for a fact that his heart was halfway up his throat for at least thirty seconds after he got back to his own time.

When his heart returned to its rightful spot, and he became more aware of his arms and legs and his hands started feeling like hands again, Scott inched away from the VCR. It took an act of pure courage to move his fingers away from the fast-forward button, but the fear of what Kelly or his parents might say if they found him standing like that gave him the strength to move.

As soon as he did, Scott became aware that he'd better sit down if he knew what was good for him. He made it to the sofa and then he collapsed. In a minute he'd have to get back up, he knew, get back into his pajamas, and try to fall asleep.

But for the minute, he sat on the sofa and allowed himself to think of nothing but the six magic numbers. Two, eight, nine, seventeen, forty-four, and forty-eight. Separately the numbers were worthless, but together they meant forty-five million dollars.

CHAPTER **9**

Two, eight, nine, seventeen, forty-four, forty-eight.

Scott chanted the numbers as he climbed the stairs back to his bedroom. He sang them again and again as he got out of his clothes and put his pajamas back on. He thought of nothing else as he crawled into bed, happy beyond belief to find his body resting between sheets again. Two, eight, nine, seventeen, forty-four, forty-eight.

And then, just to be on the safe side, he got out of bed, found a sheet of paper, and wrote the sacred numbers down. It was always possible that if he fell asleep, he'd wake up having forgotten them. If they were the winning numbers, then he could destroy the evidence. He might even eat the paper. He'd seen that in a spy movie once and had wondered ever since what paper tasted like.

Scott got back in bed and, much to his surprise, fell back asleep almost immediately. Time travel took a lot out of you, but he never suspected how much. Or maybe traveling in the future was simply more exhausting than traveling in the past.

When Scott woke up again, it was after nine, and he could tell from the sounds in the house that he was the last one up. Two, eight, nine, seventeen, forty-four, forty-eight, he thought to himself, and grinned that he still remembered the numbers. But he remembered everything about his trip in time, even when he fell trying to fly. And he would have been just as happy to forget all about that incident.

"Hi, Scott," his mother said as he walked into the kitchen. "You slept late this morning."

Scott nodded. "Did I miss anything?" he asked.

His mother shook her head. She was sitting at the kitchen table working on the crossword puzzle in the paper. Scott smiled to himself at the sight. "What would you like for breakfast?" she asked him.

"Cereal and milk," he said. "I can make it myself."

"Fine," his mother said. "I need a six-letter word for *jealous*. Do you have one on you?"

"I'll check my pockets," Scott said, but he came up empty handed. He and his mother laughed. It was an old joke between them.

"Did you sleep well last night?" his mother asked him.

"Fine," Scott replied. "Like a rock."

"Good," his mother said. "I thought I heard some

prowling around this morning, but Kelly says she slept through the night too. I guess I dreamed it."

"Guess so," Scott said. He poured out the cereal and milk and brought it to the kitchen table.

"Kelly's at her soccer game," Scott's mother declared. "Dad took her. After the game they're going out for some shopping and lunch. Kelly's been complaining about not spending enough time with Dad lately."

"So you have the morning off," Scott said.

"I only wish," his mother replied. "I have a batch of boring errands to run. Clothes to the dry cleaner's, books to the library, that sort of thing. I don't suppose I could talk you into coming with me? I'd love the company."

Under ordinary circumstances it might have irritated Scott that Kelly got to go shopping and have lunch out with their father, while he was stuck going to the dry cleaner with their mother, but today it couldn't have made him happier. "Sure, why not," he said, so he wouldn't sound too eager. "Beats doing my homework."

"You'll still have your homework to do," his mother pointed out. "But it occurred to me that when we were out, we might stop by the bakery and see what they have in the way of cookies."

Scott grinned. It was great the way his mother thought she'd have to bribe him to do the one thing he really wanted to do that day, spend time alone with her. Forty-five million dollars and an oversized chocolate-chip cookie, plus the constant pleasant glow inside of knowing he was the first person in the universe probably, and in his family definitely, to travel ahead in time. Lousy as the week before had been, this Saturday was a million times better.

He finished his cereal and rinsed his plate out, while his mother continued working on the crossword puzzle. When he was finished, he told his mother, and she got her bag and jacket. Scott walked over to the hall closet to get his, but found it wasn't there.

He had a quick moment of panic, but then he remembered taking it off in his bedroom before falling asleep. "I have to go upstairs for a minute," he told his mother, and raced up the stairs two at a time. Sure enough, his jacket was on the floor by his bed. Scott breathed a sigh of relief. It would be hard to explain to anybody if he'd left his jacket somewhere on Sunday.

"Ready, Scott?" his mother asked. "Let's get this show on the road."

So Scott joined his mother at the front door. "Let's walk," she said. "It's too nice a day to be cooped up in the car."

"Okay," Scott said. His mother handed him a carrying bag with four books in it, and she draped a couple of dresses and a suit over her left arm.

"Dry cleaner first," she said. "No reason for the entire world to see our wardrobes."

"Dry cleaner first," Scott agreed. He and his mother walked the two blocks to the dry cleaner and talked about what was happening in school. Scott told her about a couple of new kids in his class, and his mother seemed interested enough. He wondered if she had any sense that they were just killing time until that moment when they got to buy the lottery ticket and change their lives.

But his mother seemed to think going to the dry cleaner was momentous enough. She dropped the clothes on the counter and talked with the dry cleaner about spots and stains and probable return times. Scott stood around and stared at the shop. Tomorrow, when his family became rich, he supposed they'd hire someone to pick up the dresses and suit for them. Either that or they'd donate all their old clothes to charity and buy completely new wardrobes for themselves. His mother would like that, he knew. If he needed another selling point on the lottery ticket, he'd use it.

"Now the library," his mother said. "Do you want to take any books out, or are we just returning?"

"I'm still reading a book," Scott replied. "It's about a kid who travels through time on a spaceship."

"Sounds good," his mother said. "Are you enjoying it?"

"I guess so," Scott said. "It doesn't seem very realistic to me."

"You would know," his mother said. "You travel around in time every day."

Scott stood absolutely still and stared at his mother.

"That was a joke," his mother said. "Only kidding. Remember jokes? One person says something funny, and the other person goes ha-ha."

"Ha-ha," Scott said. "Yeah, it's coming back to me." He was stunned to find himself shaking.

"I'd like to travel through time," his mother declared. "There are so many things I'd like to see. The signing of the Declaration of Independence. Marie Antoinette's hair."

"Time travel isn't like that," Scott said.

"Oh," his mother said. "What is it like?"

Scott almost began explaining, and then realized how incredibly stupid that would be. "It isn't like that in this book anyway," he said. "It's about this guy, and he has a spaceship, and when he's on it, he can travel into the future. And in the future there was a big war, and he has to save his family, I mean the people who'll be his family three hundred years from now. Nobody cares about hair in the future."

"They will always care about hair," his mother said. "Hair is a constant in history. I guess I won't take any books out, either, then. I'm still reading that biography of Helen Keller."

"Does Dad want anything?" Scott asked.

"He told me to check to see if the new Richard Kramer book is in," his mother replied. "The library probably has twenty copies of it, but they're all on reserve, so I doubt we'll find one."

"Dad really would like hardbacks," Scott said. "That way he could read whatever he wants as soon as it comes out."

"He doesn't mind waiting," his mother said. They entered the library together. Scott put the books on the return desk, and his mother checked the new-fiction section to see if there were any copies of the Richard Kramer novel available. She shook her head at Scott, and they left the library.

"Maybe next week," she said. "I suppose I could have reserved it for him, but that takes the challenge away."

"Bakery next?" Scott asked.

"Bakery next," his mother replied. "The question is, do we want to eat our cookies before or after lunch?"

"How about one before, and one after," Scott suggested.

"I have an even better idea," his mother said. "One before, one after, and one during."

"How about one before, two during, one after, and then one for dessert tonight?" Scott said.

"How about if we never eat anything but cookies again," his mother said. "Cookies for breakfast and lunch and supper for the rest of our lives."

"Sounds good," Scott said. "But what about your bikinis?"

"What bikinis?" his mother asked.

"The ones you're going to wear when you win the lottery," Scott said, hoping he sounded innocent and appealing.

"The lottery," his mother said. "How about if we buy ourselves a ticket."

"You mean it?" Scott asked. He'd thought he was going to have to spend a minimum of five minutes talking his mother into it.

"Sure, why not," his mother said. "It'll be our little secret. We'll never win, so we won't have to tell your father. Let's blow the dollar just for the fun of it."

"Great," Scott said. "It's two games for a dollar, you know. Can I do one?"

"You're feeling lucky today?" his mother asked.

Scott nodded. His mother had no idea just how lucky he was feeling. "Fifty cents' worth of lucky," he said. "Look, Mom, that store sells lottery tickets."

"Oh, no, let's buy it at Pop's," his mother said.

"Pop's," Scott said.

"Sure," his mother said. "It's bound to be even luckier if we buy it there."

"But, Mom," Scott said, wishing he could come up with a valid reason why they shouldn't buy the ticket at Pop's. "I bet Pop'll be so busy, he won't want to sell us just a lottery ticket."

"That's okay," his mother said. "I want to get a couple of magazines too. I'll buy them there. Come on, Scott. Lottery tickets and magazines and then it's off to the bakery."

Scott followed his mother to Pop's store. He tried to calculate the odds on Pop figuring out that he had traveled into the future to learn the winning numbers. Given the fact Pop didn't completely believe in the VCR anyway, Scott reckoned he was safe, but he still would have preferred buying the ticket elsewhere.

But then he realized that no matter where they bought the ticket, Pop would find out they'd won the forty-five million. That wasn't the kind of thing you could keep your next-door neighbor from learning. And Pop had said selling the winning ticket would help his business out as well. So there was no point not buying the ticket at Pop's, and maybe a little bit of a point buying it there after all.

"Wait up," Scott said to his mother. She had her woman-with-a-mission look, and all of a sudden Scott realized his mother was looking forward to buying that ticket and taking her chances at forty-five million. He couldn't blame her.

"Hi, Pop," his mother said as they entered the store. "We're here to buy a lottery ticket and win ourselves all that money."

"Forty-five million," Scott said.

"Forty-two million," Pop corrected him. "What's the matter, forty-two million isn't enough for you anymore?"

Scott bit his tongue. Nobody else knew the prize money was going to go up another three million. "I got carried away," Scott said. "Forty-two, forty-five, forty-eight. Anything in front of million is good enough for me."

"You wait in line while I pick out the magazines," his mother said to him. There were already a half-dozen people standing there, waiting for their chance at the big prize money. Scott felt a moment's pang watching them filling out their cards, knowing they weren't going to win. But then again, he had no control over the numbers they picked. It wasn't his fault if none of them wrote down the right numbers. He wasn't whispering twelves and thirty-twos in their ears. They were destined to lose no matter what he did.

Still, he felt relieved when his mother joined him at the front of the line. By then another half-dozen people were standing behind them, and Scott could see even more walking into the store.

"Here's the ticket," Pop said. "Fill in the numbers you think are going to win."

Scott's mother took the ticket and gave Scott half.

"Don't tell me what your numbers are," she said. "I woke up this morning with some numbers in my head, and I just have a feeling that they're lucky. If yours are completely different, it'll worry me."

"Okay, Mom," Scott said. He stared at the ticket and took out a pen to color the little boxes with. And for one terrifying moment he couldn't remember any of the winning numbers. He couldn't even remember what a number looked like. How could he possibly win forty-five million dollars if he no longer remembered what a two was, or a seventeen?

But just saying those numbers to himself in his panic calmed Scott down. Two was one of the winning numbers, and so was seventeen. He colored in those two boxes and felt instant relief. The magic numbers came back to him. Two, eight, nine, seventeen, forty-four, and forty-eight. Two and seventeen were taken care of, so he carefully filled in the other four boxes, and stared at the card that was going to make his family rich beyond its wildest dreams.

CHAPTER 10

"I don't believe this," Scott's mother said as she and Scott's father got their jackets out of the closet. "I've heard of last-minute, but this is ridiculous."

"It's my fault too," Scott's father said. "Amy invited me a couple of days ago, and I said yes without asking you."

"That would be fine," Scott's mother said, "if you'd remembered to tell me."

"We'll have a good time," Scott's father said. "And we didn't have anything else planned for tonight anyway."

"You have no idea how lucky you are," Scott's mother said.

Scott's father didn't look like he felt lucky at all. "I'll start the car," he said, and left the house.

"I hate leaving the two of you without a baby-sitter," Scott's mother said to him and Kelly. "But when your father chooses to tell me at six forty-five that we're invited for dinner at seven-thirty, there really isn't time to make plans."

"We'll be okay, Mom," Kelly declared.

"Just follow the rules," her mother said. "Don't leave the house unless it's on fire, in which case you are to leave immediately. Don't set the house on fire, don't answer the door or the phone. If we call you, we'll ring once, hang up, and ring again, so you'll know it's us. And don't kill each other just because we're giving you the chance."

"We promise," Scott said.

"I don't believe this," his mother said. "All I wanted to do tonight was watch a movie, read a little, and see whether we won the lottery."

"The paper'll have the results tomorrow," Scott said, feeling that thrill he had enjoyed all day. "Maybe by this time tomorrow you'll be forty-two million dollars richer."

"I heard on the news it's up to forty-five," his mother said. "That's what you said at Pop's, isn't it?"

"I said forty-eight," Scott replied fast.

"What lottery?" Kelly asked. "Did you two buy lottery tickets?"

"Just a dollar's worth," her mother said. "Watch the drawing and write the numbers down for me, before you go to bed. We'll be home by midnight. And call Miri's mother if you have any problems. She knows you're here alone, so she's on call."

Scott's father honked the horn. Scott's mother sighed and ran out of the house.

"I don't believe you talked Mom into buying a lottery ticket," Kelly said. "I tried to persuade Dad, but he wouldn't budge."

"It was Tahiti," Scott replied. "And the bikinis."

"It would be great if we won," Kelly said. "Not likely, but great."

"Someone has to win," Scott said. "It might be us."

"We have the VCR," Kelly declared. "I think that's as lucky as we're going to get."

Scott tried not to grin. "What do you want to do tonight?" he asked, figuring a change in subject was a good idea. "I think Mom threw out *Sinsational Lust.*"

"I don't know," Kelly said. "I guess we could watch TV."

"Okay," Scott said. He turned the set on, and they watched a couple of shows.

"This is boring," Kelly declared after a particularly bad sitcom. "I'm tired of TV. Let's do something else for a while."

"Just as long as we remember to watch the lottery drawing," Scott said. "That's on at ten."

"We'll remember," Kelly said. "Let's play a game."

"Like what?" Scott asked.

"Clue, maybe," Kelly said. "Or Career. I don't care what. Just something I can beat you at."

"I'll bet you a million trillion dollars I win," Scott said.

"You're on," Kelly said. "Do I get to pick the game?"

"I can beat you at anything," Scott said.

"Fine," Kelly said. "The games are in your room, right?"

"In my closet," Scott said.

"I'll go up and pick one," Kelly said. "Meanwhile you figure out where you're going to get a million trillion dollars." She left the living room and walked upstairs.

Scott grinned. He might not be able to come up with the trillion, but the million was right around the corner. He'd even let Kelly have it, once he'd won. There was no point being selfish when you had forty-five million dollars.

He went into the kitchen and filled a bowl with popcorn while he waited for his sister. Tomorrow he'd go out and buy a whole new set of bowls. They'd be made of solid gold, and he'd fill them with popcorn and potato chips and eat as much as he wanted. Then, instead of washing the bowls out, he'd throw them away and buy a whole new set of golden bowls. Or maybe silver next time. He'd let his mother decide. After all, technically speaking, the forty-five million was hers, since she paid the dollar to buy the ticket.

Scott had a moment of panic thinking that maybe his mother would decide all the money really was hers, and not let him have any fun with it. But that seemed so unlikely, he decided not to worry. His mother was always telling him and Kelly to share, mostly to stop them from screaming at each other. She could hardly refuse to share with him, especially when he had been the one to pick the numbers.

"Scott," Kelly said, as she walked down the stairs. She

was holding a couple of games, but she was also carefully balancing a piece of paper on the top of the game boxes.

"Yeah, Kel," Scott said. "You pick the game?"

"I couldn't decide," she said. "Scott, there was a piece of paper right by your bed with some numbers written on it."

"Numbers," Scott said, and then he remembered. They were his lottery ticket numbers. "Yeah, what about it?"

"I was just wondering what they meant," Kelly said. "Two, eight, nine, seventeen, forty-four, forty-eight."

Scott thought about lying, but realized there was no point. In a couple of hours they'd be picking those numbers on television. There was no way of keeping Kelly from finding out the winning numbers, and with her memory she'd be sure to recognize them when they were called out.

"They're my lottery ticket numbers," Scott said.

"Your lottery ticket numbers?" Kelly said. "I thought Mom bought the ticket."

"She did," Scott said. "And she filled out half, and I filled out the other half. I don't know what numbers she chose, but those were my numbers."

"So why did you write them down?" Kelly asked. "Don't you have your half of the ticket?"

"Sure," Scott said. "I wrote them down so I wouldn't forget them."

"How could you forget them if you had them on your ticket?" Kelly said.

"Before I bought the ticket," Scott said. "You know, not everybody buys a ticket and decides what numbers to pick there. Mom knew the numbers she was going to choose before she bought her ticket, and I knew my numbers too."

"You cared enough about these numbers to write them down beforehand?" Kelly asked.

"They're special numbers," Scott muttered. "They felt lucky to me."

"I'll bet they did," Kelly said. "All right, Scott. What's going on?"

"What do you mean?" Scott asked.

Kelly flung the games on the floor. The boxes opened, and pieces of both games flew out. Paper money scattered all over the room. Scott wondered if forty-five million dollars had just fallen out.

"What did you say at Pop's?" Kelly asked. "About how many million the lottery was going to be worth?"

"What difference does it make?" Scott asked.

"Scott!" Kelly screeched. "Stop acting dumb and tell me what you did to win the lottery."

"What makes you think I won?" Scott asked.

"You're going to tell me you didn't?" Kelly asked. "You're going to tell me when they pick the numbers they're not going to be two and eight and nine and seventeen and forty-four and forty-eight?"

"How should I know?" Scott asked.

"That's what I'm trying to find out," Kelly replied. "How you found out. Is this all past time or something? Have we already lived through Saturday night and it's actually Sunday and you reset the VCR so you could go back and buy the right ticket?"

"How could I do that?" Scott asked. "If I set the

machine so I could buy the winning ticket, then why would I set it again just to live through Saturday night again?"

"Shut up," Kelly said, sitting down on the sofa. "You're giving me a headache."

So Scott kept quiet. Kelly kicked off her shoes, bit down on her lip, and thought.

"Oh, Scott, you didn't," she said.

"No, I didn't," he said automatically. "Didn't what?"

"You did," Kelly said. "I'll bet that's just what you did. You went ahead in time to find out the winning numbers."

"No, I didn't," Scott said. "Honest."

"You're such a fibber," Kelly said. "What did it feel like, going ahead in time?"

"Like going back, only worse," Scott said. "But once you're there, it feels the same."

"I've got to do it," Kelly said. "Just once. It's really safe?"

"I'm here, aren't I?" Scott said.

"I think so," Kelly replied. "Lately it's been getting hard to tell."

"I figured we could definitely sell the VCR to the Pentagon if it could go into the future," Scott said. "And you'd be sure to win your Nobel Prize."

"I bet you're right," Kelly said. "But, Scott. You actually went ahead in time to find out the winning lottery ticket numbers?"

"This morning," Scott said. "I went ahead to tomorrow and read the numbers in the paper. Only, the article said the prize had gone up to forty-five million. And when Mom bought the ticket at Pop's, I let it slip."

"Forty-five million dollars," Kelly said. "Dad would die."

"He'll adjust," Scott declared.

"Not if he finds out how you won it," Kelly said.

"Then he won't find out," Scott said. "We don't have to tell him anything, except that Mom bought a ticket. That we can't keep from him."

"If we don't tell him eventually, I won't be able to win my Nobel Prize," Kelly pointed out. "And you won't be able to sell the machine to the Pentagon."

"We'll think of something," Scott said. "We can always tell him we didn't find out about the VCR until after we won the lottery."

"I don't know," Kelly said. "It seems to me you're doing a lot of lying already."

"No, I'm not," Scott said.

"Wait a second," Kelly said. "You bought the ticket at Pop's?"

Scott nodded.

"Great," Kelly said. "Real bright, Scott."

"It was Mom's idea," Scott said.

"Pop knows about the VCR," Kelly said. "What if he figures out what you did?"

"I don't think he will," Scott said, starting to feel uncomfortable. "Besides, he doesn't really believe in it."

"He will once we sell it to the Pentagon," Kelly said. "And he'll know exactly when we figured out how the VCR really works. So he'll tell Dad, and Dad'll realize how you won the lottery, and then I don't know what he'll do, but I know you won't like it."

"Come on," Scott said. "There's got to be a way to make all this work."

"I don't see how," Kelly replied. "If Pop didn't know, then maybe. But he does and even if he doesn't go to the governor and tell her what happened, he'll be sure to tell Mom and Dad. And you know them. If they even think it's cheating, they'll get mad."

"Do you think it's cheating?" Scott asked his sister.

Kelly nodded. "I'm sorry, Scott," she said. "The idea was brilliant, and I wish I'd been the first to travel in the future, but it's cheating. It's like getting a copy of a test before the teacher gives it, so you can look the answers up and get a hundred."

"It isn't a hundred," Scott said. "It's forty-five million dollars."

"Don't remind me," Kelly said. "I'm throwing away the chance to be the richest only child in the world."

"How do you figure that?" Scott asked.

"Because Mom and Dad'll kill you when they find out what you did," Kelly said. "I don't suppose you love me enough to sacrifice your life so I can be insanely, incredibly rich."

"The idea was for me to be that rich," Scott told her. "Well, what do I do now?"

"You could tear the ticket up," Kelly said. "Just tell Mom you didn't pick the right numbers and no one'll be any the wiser."

"I am not tearing forty-five million dollars up," Scott declared. "Forget it, Kelly."

"You can't keep it," Kelly said. "So I guess you might as well give it away."

"Give away forty-five million dollars?" Scott sputtered, his face turning crimson. "Who should I give it to? You?"

Kelly giggled. "I only wish," she said. "I think you'd better give it away to someone who won't suspect anything. Is there anyone you like well enough to slip them forty-five million?"

Scott shook his head.

"It's a shame we can't travel really far into the future," Kelly said. "Then you could find out who you're going to marry and you could give her the ticket now so when you got married, you'd be really rich."

"But if we got a divorce, she'd get to keep all the money," Scott said. "And she might spend it all before I married her."

"In that case you just wouldn't marry her," Kelly said. "But it doesn't matter. I think you should give the ticket away to a group or something. Some place that'll spend the money to help people."

"Like to cure cancer?" Scott asked.

"Like that," Kelly said. "Only a group that really needs the money. Everybody gives money to cure cancer."

Scott stared at Kelly, who stared right back. "The victims group!" they both said.

"We can slip the ticket under their door," Kelly said. "And then they can use the money to help more people."

"But let's wait until after we know for sure the numbers really did win," Scott said.

Kelly nodded. "We'll wrap the ticket up in an anonymous letter," she said. "We'll cut the words out of the paper, just like a ransom note."

"I'll get the newspaper," Scott said. By the time he came out of the kitchen, Kelly had already gotten paper, paste, and a scissors. "Short and sweet," she said. "And we should wear gloves, so they won't find our fingerprints."

"Okay," Scott said. They worked on it together and eventually turned out a note that said, *This Is the Winning Lottery ticket. Spend it to Help Victims.* In his opinion, at least, the note looked professional.

"Now all we have to do is see if you won," Kelly said.

"Let's turn the TV on now," Scott said.

Kelly nodded. She turned the TV on, and they sat together watching show after show until finally the lottery drawing was announced.

"My stomach hurts," Kelly said, but Scott wasn't able to say anything. He felt even sicker than he had traveling into the future. In a matter of moments he was going to win and lose forty-five million dollars.

A woman came on the air and said, "I'm drawing for the largest lottery in this state's history. First prize is at least forty-two million dollars."

"We know already," Scott muttered. "Get on with it."

The woman pushed Ping-Pong balls around. "The first number is eight," she declared. "Number eight for the forty-two-million-dollar prize." She lifted another Ping-

Pong ball, looked at it, and said, "The second number is seventeen."

Kelly and Scott recited the numbers along with her. It took her a little under a minute to announce the six winning numbers, numbers the twins already knew by heart.

"Giving the ticket away is the right thing to do," Kelly said softly after they turned the set off. "And you'll get the money back when you sell the VCR to the Pentagon. Only then it'll be legal."

"I know," Scott said. "But wouldn't it have been great?"

Kelly nodded. "It would have been super great," she said. "Almost as great as being the first person to ever travel ahead in time."

CHAPTER **11**

Scott wasn't the least bit worried about waking up before dawn on this real Sunday morning. He hardly slept at all that night, so it was no trick to get out of bed at five-thirty.

It was hard to fall asleep when he knew he owned the winning lottery ticket but wasn't going to keep it. Scott didn't know of another human being who would be able to sleep under those circumstances.

He heard his parents get in close to midnight, but he pretended to be sleeping when they opened his door and peeked in on him. The last thing he wanted just then was to explain his insomnia to them. His parents went to bed and, as far as Scott knew, slept through the night. Why shouldn't they? They didn't know about the fortune spending the night wrapped inside an anonymous note, and hiding under his pillow.

At five-thirty Scott gave up and got out of bed. He put on the clothes he'd worn the day before, and with shaking hands put the ticket in his pants pocket. He tiptoed out of his room and went downstairs, where he found Kelly, fully dressed, sleeping on the living room sofa.

"Oh, hi," she said, yawning mightily as he walked toward her.

"What are you doing up?" Scott asked.

"I thought you might want company," she said.

"You mean you wanted to make sure I actually did it," Scott said.

Kelly shook her head. "I know you will," she said. "Because it's the right thing and because it's the smart thing. I just figured you wouldn't want to do it alone."

"You're right," Scott said, relieved that Kelly had volunteered to accompany him. "But hurry. We want to do it now, before anybody shows up there."

"That's why I'm dressed," Kelly said. They walked over to the closet, got their jackets, and left the house, closing the front door as quietly as they could manage. "Was the day like this yesterday?" she asked Scott as they began their walk. "When you went ahead to today."

"The weather was the same," Scott said. "I felt different, though."

"I bet," Kelly said. "Scott, we can sell the VCR and get at least forty-five million for it. You can be as rich as you want."

"Do you want to sell it?" Scott asked.

"No," Kelly replied. "I'm not even ready to tell Mom and Dad. I want to have some more adventures with it first."

"Me too," Scott said. "Besides, what would I do with forty-five million dollars?"

"Spend it on baseball cards?" Kelly asked.

"Right," Scott said. "And comic books."

"The victims group will do good stuff with the money," Kelly said. "They'll help people like Pop."

Scott nodded. "I know all that," he said. "And I know I'm doing the best thing. And maybe someday I'll figure out another way to use the VCR to get lots of money. So now can we stop talking about it?"

"I won't say another word," Kelly declared, and much to Scott's surprise she kept her word. In silence they walked to the building the crime victims group rented. Scott was pleased to have her company, and walking in the early morning light also improved his mood. Sure, he was giving away forty-five million dollars. But how many people could say that? At some point he'd tell someone what he'd done, and the look of shock and respect in that person's eyes would be every bit as good as having the greatest baseball-card collection in the universe.

"There it is," Kelly said, pointing the building out to Scott. "Do you think we should put the ticket in the mailbox?"

Scott shook his head. "They won't look there until the mail gets delivered on Monday," he said. "And in the meantime somebody might steal the ticket. No, let's slip it under the door."

So they walked up the steps. Scott began shaking

again, and once they got to the top of the steps, he didn't know if he was going to be able to stop.

And then Kelly did an amazing thing. She gave Scott an enormous hug and kissed him on his cheek. "I think you're terrific," she declared. "Now do it."

And Scott did. He took the note out of his pocket, checked to see that the ticket was wrapped in it, and pushed note and ticket under the door. The twins stood on tiptoe and looked through the high window on the door. Sure enough, the note was on the floor, where someone was bound to find it.

"Let's go," Scott said. "Fast."

He and Kelly ran all the way home. Running helped, Scott found. When he was busy moving one foot ahead of the other, it was almost impossible to think about what he had just done.

They got back home as dawn was breaking. "Do you think you can sleep now?" Kelly asked him as they walked upstairs to their bedrooms.

Scott shook his head. "I don't think I'll ever sleep again," he declared, but he kicked off his shoes and crawled into bed. And within seconds he was sound asleep.

By the time he woke up, it was close to ten, and he could hear lots of noise in the house. Scott had to think for a second to remember what had happened, but when he did, he turned his radio to the local station, to see if there was any news about the ticket.

And boy, was there. It was the lead story on the ten A.M. news broadcast. Scott rested against his pillow and listened to what they had to say.

"This morning the State Lottery Commission announced that there was only one winning lottery ticket sold for yesterday's record-setting forty-five-million-dollar jackpot," the announcer declared. "And that ticket was purchased right here at Pop Horowitz's Candy Shop on the corner of Lexington and Fourth."

Scott grinned. Pop couldn't have bought a better commercial. He hoped Pop's business tripled, at least for a week or two.

"But the story gets even more interesting," the announcer said. "Because whoever bought that winning ticket has chosen to donate it anonymously to the local Crime Victims Association. Mr. David Letchworth, head of the organization, found the ticket slipped under the door, less than an hour ago, when he opened the building for its Sunday meetings. WVRC was the first radio station to see the note that accompanied the ticket. It said, and we quote, *This is the winning lottery ticket. Spend it to help victims.* So whoever gave away that forty-five-million-dollar slip of paper knew exactly what he or she was doing."

Scott nodded. He certainly did know what he had done, and for the first time he kind of liked the fact that he'd done it.

"We have Mr. Letchworth here at our studio," the radio announcer declared. "Mr. Letchworth, you must be in a very good mood this morning."

"I'm in a state of shock," Mr. Letchworth said. Scott liked the way the man sounded. He stretched out in his bed and thought about how Mr. Letchworth must have looked when he found the ticket and note waiting for him.

"What did you do when you first found the ticket?" the announcer asked.

"I ran to the local newsstand and bought a paper," Mr. Letchworth replied. "To confirm that it was indeed the winning ticket. And it was. All six numbers were the same. So then I called Janis Myers. She's a lawyer who works with the Crime Victims Association."

"And what was her advice?" the announcer asked.

"It was hard to tell," Mr. Letchworth said. "Because when I told her, she began to laugh and cry, and frankly, so did I. When we both calm down, we'll get together and talk about it rationally."

"And in the meantime?" the announcer said.

"In the meantime we've handed the ticket over to the local police to guard for us," Mr. Letchworth said. "And we called the Lottery Commission to say we'd be claiming the prize money."

"Forty-five million dollars is a lot of money," the radio announcer declared. Scott grinned. That was hardly news. "Have you been able to make any plans?"

"We're going to be able to realize a lot of dreams," Mr. Letchworth declared. "For starters we're going to open a shelter for victims of domestic crimes. We need a home for women whose husbands have been beating them. We've been applying for grants for years now without any luck. And now we don't have to beg for charity anymore. We can take care of our own."

"Any other plans?" the announcer asked.

"Not yet," Mr. Letchworth said. "Whoever entrusted

this money to us knew we would spend it carefully to help victims. And that's our intention."

"Do you have any words for the charitable individual who gave you the ticket?" the announcer asked.

"Thank you," Mr. Letchworth declared. "When I've calmed down a little, I'm sure I'll be able to say it better, but right now all I can do is say thank you. I don't know who you are, but you're a remarkable person and you've done more good than you can even begin to imagine."

"That's David Letchworth, head of the local Crime Victims Association," the radio announcer declared. "For those of you who just tuned in, an anonymous donor gave this week's forty-five-million-dollar lottery ticket to the organization."

Scott turned off the radio. David Letchworth sounded like a nice guy, and Scott liked the way he didn't rattle off ten thousand different things he was going to do with the money. They should think about how to spend it for a while, he decided. That kind of money shouldn't just be frittered away.

Scott got dressed and went downstairs. He found his parents, Kelly, Miri, and Pop all in the living room.

"We thought you'd never wake up," his mother said. "The most amazing thing's happened."

"What?" Scott asked, deliberately avoiding looking at Kelly.

"Pop sold someone the winning lottery ticket," his mother said. "It was worth forty-five million, and whoever bought it gave it to the Crime Victims group. The one Pop told us about the other evening."

"You're kidding," Scott said, and yawned. It was either yawning or laughing, and yawning was the safer thing to do.

"Pop, do you have any idea who could have bought the ticket?" Scott's mother asked.

Pop shook his head. "I sold hundreds of tickets all week," he declared. "It could have been anybody. Even the mayor bought five tickets."

"I know the mayor," Scott's father said. "He wouldn't donate the time of day, let alone forty-five million dollars."

"What I don't get is why they gave it to the Crime Victims," Scott's mother said. "It's so odd that whoever bought the ticket at Pop's gave the money to a group Pop's involved with. It's almost like a tribute to him."

"It's probably just a coincidence," Pop declared, and gave Scott a look so knowing that Scott had to turn away from his gaze. "But it's going to be great for my business that the ticket was bought there, so tribute or no, I'm grateful."

"And I'm hungry," Miri said. "We're all going out for pancakes to celebrate," she told Scott. "Mom's drying her hair, but she should be finished in a few minutes, and then we'll go."

"Sounds great," Scott said.

"I need to escape from the phone calls," Pop declared. "The phone's been ringing all morning long, since they announced that the ticket was bought at my store. And when they found out the ticket got given away, it's been even worse."

"The world loves a mystery," Scott's mother said. "And this is a special sort of mystery."

"I have to agree," Scott's father said. "Somewhere in this town there's a very special person. Someone without greed, someone capable of giving away a fortune to help others. I'd like to meet that person someday."

Scott risked a look at Kelly. "I think there must have been two people involved, Dad," he said.

"Two," his father replied. "What makes you say that?"

"Because I don't think one person would have had the strength to give that kind of money away," Scott said. "I know I wouldn't have."

Kelly smiled at him. Scott couldn't remember ever having felt as good as he did just then.

"I bet you're right, Scott," his father said. "There are two remarkable people in this town, then."

"There's more than two," Scott's mother said. "Just in this room there are six remarkable people."

"Remarkably hungry," Kelly said. "Come on, Miri. Let's go to your house and speed things up."

"Good thinking," Miri said, and the two girls raced out of the house to go next door.

"Maybe they'll name the new shelter for you, Pop," Scott's father said. "You can represent the anonymous donor."

"I'd be honored to," Pop said. "You know, I'm starting to believe in guardian angels. Someone out there is being more than generous to me lately."

Scott's mother stood up and gave Pop a kiss on the forehead. "You deserve it," she said. "Come on, Scott. Help me bring these mugs into the kitchen."

So Scott gathered coffee mugs and followed his

mother. There was no way she could know what had happened, he told himself, as he began to panic. But she hardly needed his help to carry three mugs from one room to the next.

"I wanted to get you alone," she whispered to him.

How could she know? Scott asked himself. And if she did know, how should he behave? As far as he could tell, he hadn't done anything wrong, but maybe his mother wouldn't see it that way. Scott put the two mugs in the sink and waited to hear what his mother had to say.

"I won the lottery!" she whispered.

"You what?" Scott asked.

"Well, not the whole thing," she said. "Actually, all I got was four numbers right, but that's worth ninety-eight dollars and twelve cents according to the radio."

"Mom, that's great," Scott said, and he held on to the sink to keep from collapsing right in front of his mother.

"I told you I woke up yesterday with those numbers in my head," his mother said. "And the funny thing was, I kept hearing them in your voice. Two and eight and nine and seventeen. There were other numbers, too, but I couldn't quite make them out. So I used those four numbers and a couple of others I thought I could hear, and sure enough those four were on the winning ticket."

Scott remembered how he'd walked up the stairs Saturday morning muttering the numbers over and over again, and wished he'd muttered all six of them just a little bit louder.

"What are you going to do with the money?" he asked.

"That's up to you," his mother said. "I figure I

MAR
MAR 3

ABOUT THE AUTHOR

SUSAN BETH PFEFFER is the author of many books for young readers, including *Courage, Dana; Just Between Us;* and *What Do You Do When Your Mouth Won't Open? Future Forward* follows *Rewind to Yesterday* as the second of two books about time travel.

Ms. Pfeffer is a native New Yorker who now lives in Middletown, New York.

wouldn't have bought the ticket except for you. What do you want to do with it?"

"I want a dog," Scott said, no doubt in his mind.

"You're on," his mother said. "We'll go to the pet store this afternoon and spend my winnings on a dog."

"Can we get one at the animal shelter instead?" Scott asked. "A stray no one else wants? We can use the ninety-eight dollars and twelve cents for a collar and license."

Scott's mother walked over to Scott and gave him a big hug. "Can we call him Lucky?" she asked. "Because right now I feel like I'm the luckiest person in the world."

Scott nodded. "Lucky's fine with me," he said, realizing that his mother was only the second luckiest person in the world. "Let's adopt a Lucky dog."